I0742932

Two Parts Demon
An Obscure Magic Book 2

By

Viola Grace

Benny has completed the XIA course that will let her work with the agents she became close to while hunting a serial killer. It will take effect the moment they are cleared of demonic influence. Nothing like knowing that your blood is despised to make a girl feel wanted.

After a night on the town with Freddy, Benny runs into the agents, and they are not only hogging her favourite taco joint, but they are interested in her social status. She is about to say yes to whatever they can come up with when she gets a call from her house, and the night goes downhill from there.

Karaoke, kidnapping and binding spells make up the rest of the night when Benny must head to the demon zone and Argyle, Smith and Tremble refuse to let her go alone.

Nothing like jumping into a dimensional prison to lock in a first date.

The characters and events in this book are fictitious. Any similarity to real persons, living or dead, is coincidental and not intended by the author.

Published by Viola Grace

Look for me online at violagrace.com, amazon, kobo, B&N and other ebook sellers.

$\mathcal{B}$enny grunted as she was struck from above and continued crawling through the obstacle course.

"Come on, demon. Lose it!"

Benny gritted her teeth and continued to pull herself forward, arm by arm. She really hated control training, but today was her last day. One way or another.

She scraped her belly on the rough ground of the course; her tank top was no protection against the gravel and dirt. She hissed as a boot connected with her ribs and another kick sent her tumbling. She held in her pain and kept moving until she could get to her feet and run through the swinging, weighted bags.

Benny gritted her teeth as curses and insults to her bloodline were spewed at her. This was practice for being in the field and dealing with those who were not too keen to be subdued. She wanted nothing more than to finish her training and get into the SUV with her agents, if only to get away from the trainers.

She grunted as one of the bags made impact, but kept going. She could see the end of the course.

It had been decided that the best way to prove her worth to the XIA was to go through endless rounds of stress testing. If she could keep her cool under every circumstance they could come up with, she was safe to be in public.

Her ability to use magic was not in question. She was physically capable of managing the tasks that made up the bare minimum of the staffing skills for the Extranormal Investigation Agency.

She could apply for additional training later on, but the course designed to test her skills and tolerances was her first step.

Her impulses wanted her to burn a pathway through the course, but her self-control kept her doing things the hard way.

Benny grunted and heard a distant voice call her a scaly bitch. She sighed and poured on the speed while her bruised body screamed silently.

When she stumbled across the finish line, it was time for the final task. Benny whispered and moved the pegs into the properly sized holes using tightly con-trolled magic.

The light turned green when the last peg hit the slot, and she dropped to the ground.

Her trainers applauded wildly and cheers sounded around the workout yard.

Benny looked around and nodded wearily. "So, did I pass?"

Agent Tafnor chuckled and pulled her to her feet. "You did. Time for the final photos, and then, you are officially cleared by the training centre."

Benny nodded and headed toward the imaging booth. She had been photographed every day for the last two weeks. The bruises and damage to her body were tracked for a very specific reason—she needed to know how a victim felt. She needed to know how easy it was to damage evidence on her own body, and she had to feel the exposure of the photographs.

All agents were subjected to a rape kit at some point during training. She had opted to get that out of the way on the first day. Today, it was just the indignity of stripping down in front of the camera.

A cold voice greeted her when she entered the space. "Take off your shirt."

She flinched at the aggression in the tone. Benny pulled her tank top off, exposing the damage to her upper torso. The camera flashed, and she winced at the light.

"Hold still."

The camera flashed again.

She was ordered to turn to the side and then face the back of the photo area.

"Now remove your pants."

She hesitated.

"Now!"

Benny got angrier than she had been while she had been physically attacked. The camera flashed, and she flipped her middle finger at the shadows before she removed her trousers and pushed them to her ankles, leaving her bra and panties as the only things covering her.

The cameraman got closer, but she still couldn't see him. He took close photos of her thighs, back and ribs.

"Remove your bra."

"No. You can see the damage around it. This is my body, and I am saying no."

"This is an order."

"No. This is a courtesy. This exercise is to make me feel like a victim or a suspect, and in either situation, I would ram that camera through your jaw." She pulled her cargo pants back up and pulled on her top.

"You are already healing. We needed to document the pattern."

She snorted. "I heal the same as a shifter does. I just don't match any blood types that they do. I have to be faster or I die."

Benny tucked her shirt into her pants, and she lit the interior of the photo booth with a ball of soft light. No hands required.

The goblin in the XIA uniform grimaced. "Can you turn that down?"

She dimmed the light. "You need to use manners when you deal with either suspect or victim. You were very close to breaking my control."

He chuckled. "I know. Check this out."

He turned the camera to her and showed her an image of her glaring at the camera, her eyes were poisonous green and very demonic.

"Oops."

His finger slipped and the image disappeared.

She frowned. "Why did you do that?"

"They are looking for reasons to restrict your movements. Let's not give them an excuse."

Benny cocked her head. "I will not lie about seeing my own demon in the mirror."

He inclined his head. "And so I will lie for you."

His fingers moved over the back of the camera. "Sent. Your training is now complete."

She patted him on the shoulder, a move that caught him by surprise.

Benny sighed. She knew that most of the XIA did not touch the goblins, but she didn't have any hang-ups in that regard. Their magic and transformation came from the same energy that ran in her veins. There was no difference.

Benny double-checked her clothing and left the photo area. "Thank you."

He was so stunned by her thanks that he didn't respond.

She returned to the training area and accepted congratulations for successfully making it through the course without biting her trainers. Apparently, that was a thing.

Benny just wanted to go home. Her parents had started some kind of extension on the dower house, so Benny was stuck in her old room at the big house with Jessamine haunting her day in and day out. With nowhere to be alone, she was closer to cracking at home than she was having the crap kicked out of her at work.

After the congratulations, she hit the showers and grabbed her bag. If she could manage to get changed, Freddy had asked her out for a karaoke night. Howling into a microphone was right up her current mood.

Pooky was waiting for her, and he revved up the moment she entered the parking lot. Benny flexed her swollen knuckles around the steering wheel and whispered, "Take me home."

Pooky did as he was told. He took her home at a safe and sedate speed. Her muscles were alternately tensing and twitching, so it was better that she wasn't driving.

The shower had been nice, but she was going to run around in the greenhouse the moment she got home. She was healing fast, but not fast enough to go out in a tank top. She would have enough time to administer a healing draught, but she would not be able to drink when she went out with Freddy. Given her friend's penchant for getting her into trouble, it was better that when Benny went out, she stayed sober.

Benny and Freddy leaned in close to the mic and howled along with a full-moon love song. Freddy's other form was canine, so she thought she could hit the right notes. Benny could hear Freddy's voice swing and miss over and over again.

Some of the members of the crowd had their hands over their ears, but others were listening with rapt attention. Those enjoying the music were usually of goblin descent. They enjoyed the notes that were up beyond standard hearing.

As the song concluded, Benny

laughed and leaned back, heading for a glass of water. She sat to the side as the next singer took the stage.

"Well, your voice hasn't suffered now that you are all official and stuff." Freddy grinned and slugged down her cocktail.

"I have done a lot of shouting and grunting this week. It is a bit more physically challenging than I am used to, but it keeps me busy. I think I am going to enjoy this." Benny shrugged and nodded to the waitress for another glass of water.

"We miss you at work. You used to bring in samples. The new food writer doesn't bring in samples." Freddy pouted.

It hurt to think that she had been replaced already. "That is too bad."

"You are telling me. I have had to start *paying* for food. It is horrifying."

The water and another cocktail arrived. Benny tipped the waitress and gulped down the water. It was all she had been drinking for the past week. When she needed to heal, it was water or nothing.

"So, are you still going to be driving around with those agents? The photos in the articles were extremely frustrating."

Benny grinned and sipped at her water. "Why was that, Freddy?" She already knew the answer.

"They were fully clothed."

They sat giggling as a baritone crooned a classic from the forties.

Freddy turned to her. "Do you want to do another?"

"Want to? Yes. Should I? No. I have been getting plenty of attention this week. I don't need to jump on stage."

"How are you dealing with that?"

"The freak trying to rip away my humanity or the fact that my great grandmother was behind it?"

"Both."

She didn't mention the role her parents had played. That was something that was going to be dealt with later.

"I am dealing with it. The training has helped."

Kobar came up to the table, and he slipped Benny a piece of paper. He whispered, "Please."

She looked at the song on the slip and listened to the warbling of the current singer and nodded. He walked away in relief.

Freddy looked at her with a raised eyebrow. "What was that?"

"Folks are starting to leave. He has a request."

"Well, I will leave you to it. I believe this calls for a solo." Freddy flapped her hand and waved her toward the stage.

Benny got up as the last of the song died away and took her place behind the microphone. The watchers perked up, and she began to sing a vampire love song about love and death, blood and pain, all coming together to haunt the new vampire for eternity. *Love Never Dies* was always a classic.

The few vampires in the audience were crying tears of blood by the time she finished her song.

Benny felt the same rush that she always did when the applause followed her off the stage. She finished the water that Freddy had guarded, and she waved her hand at her friend. "Come on, time to get something to eat."

"Yay!" Freddy bounced to her feet and clapped her hands.

They made their way through the crowd listening to a mage with quite a good voice. It was time to hunt down a food truck.

Chapter Two

"So, what do you feel like? Pizza? Tacos? That weird noodle thing?" Benny drove through the streets on the lookout for something edible.

"Well, you know I am always up for that weird noodle thing, but I think that tacos are our best bet tonight."

"Tacos it is. Pooky, you know the way."

The car did a quick U-turn, and Benny sat back while they were driven to the taco truck.

When they arrived and got out of the car, Benny snickered. "Well, it seems I have created addicts."

Freddy leaned against her arm. "Do

tell."

Benny linked arms with her friend and hauled her toward the picnic table occupied by Smith, Argyle and Tremble.

Two of the three men were covered in taco grease and not at their best. Benny made the introductions anyway.

"Gentlemen, you remember my best friend, Freddy. Freddy, you remember that these are the agents that turned my life upside down, Smith, Argyle and Tremble."

Freddy shook their hands and licked her palm clean afterward. Benny didn't explain, she just headed to the truck and ordered for herself and Freddy with a bright smile and a wink for Dem-rah behind the counter.

With her hands laden with tacos and juggling sodas, she headed for the table where Freddy was flirting madly with the three XIA agents.

Benny settled, and Smith pressed his

thigh against hers. "It is good to see you, Benny."

She nodded as she doused one of her victims with hot sauce. "You too, Smith. 'scuse me."

She tilted her head and found four pairs of eyes watching her. She shrugged and dived in. The spice hit her before the flavour did, and she closed her eyes and kept eating. Sweat prickled on her upper lip, but she kept going.

She opened one eye a crack when she heard Freddy starting on her own meal. Having a best friend that was part hell-hound was definitely interesting. Her table manners were always lacking, but her enthusiasm could not be denied.

Benny finished her tacos and wiped her face. Her lips throbbed with a steady beat. She daintily sipped at her soda, and the sugar sent her senses reeling.

She sat up and looked at the agents. "So, you have been declared demon free?"

Smith grinned. "Relatively. We are fit for duty."

Argyle folded his hands on the table. "How did you do in your training, Benny?"

She smirked. "I passed, though it was less training and more stress testing. They were trying to make me freak out on them."

Tremble blinked. "That is unusual. What was the purpose?"

"They seem to think that my bloodline makes me unstable. The trainers used every method they could to make me manifest my demon side. It wasn't comfortable, but I didn't flip out."

Smith chuckled. "At least it was only stress testing. They didn't hurt you."

She paused, and it was long enough for him to sprout claws and mark the table. Tremble looked shocked, but Argyle patted his friend on the shoulder and nodded. "I thought as much."

Benny chuckled. "I am glad one of us knew I would have the crap kicked out of me. They used pain, exhaustion and verbal abuse to try and make me lash out. I am happy to say that it didn't work."

Argyle nodded. "When do you report for duty?"

Benny grinned. "I have no idea. They are going to assign me as a fourth to a team. I am cleared to work, but I don't know when I start. When do you guys get to go back?"

Tremble smiled. "We are still on leave, though we have been cleared of all demon influence."

Argyle smirked. "Feel free to influence us anytime."

Benny snorted. "I am dealing with my change in circumstance. Kyria has been banned from my home, and my parents are waiting for the investigation to get to them."

Smith frowned. "Does that bother you?"

"Having to lock out one of my oldest ancestors? Yes. She was part of me, part of my family. She was the origin of the demon blood in my bloodline. It hurts to have her separate from us, but she was acting as a demon. She was focused on her wants and desires and pursuing them." Benny couldn't believe that she was having this conversation in a vacant lot next to a taco truck, but there it was.

Smith cocked his head. "Is that what the fuss was about? Is that demon influence?"

Freddy chimed in. "You don't get it. If a demoness wants to get some sleep and her baby is crying, she will kill it. If a demon male sees a woman he wants and she is with her husband or family, he will kill them to clear the path. The emotions of their victims never even enter their reckoning. They simply don't see anything but themselves."

Argyle cleared his throat. "I have wondered how it works with your parents, Benny."

Benny made a face. "Well, Dad manifested as an incubus, and he is in love with my mother. She provides him with everything he needs, and he is satisfied. His blood binds them, so he would never stray, but he does get sexually frustrated very easily, which did mean that I couldn't have sleepovers. They created a schedule that worked for all of us, and I learned to reheat things in the microwave. Eventually, I learned to cook."

Tremble leaned in, "What do you mean *manifested as an incubus*?"

"No demon is a copy of their parents. It is a random assignment of genetics and magic. Kyria is a succubus, her child was a book demon and his child was an incubus. Kyria's father is a demon king, and she definitely is not one of the ruling demon classes."

Tremble was genuinely curious. "How do you know?"

Benny smirked. "The horns. The kings have large racks like deer do. They are born with those as their crown."

Smith chimed in, "So they are automatically in charge?"

"No. They have to take down another king. It just gives them the right to pick the fight." Freddy mumbled around her taco.

Argyle glanced at Freddy. "How do you know about it?"

Freddy snorted. "One, I am Benny's best friend and have been since we were six. Two, my family has had some occupational exposure to demons in the past."

Tremble cocked his head. "Why?"

Benny took the glance that Freddy threw her. "Okay, I can see that they are more annoying than decorative. How do I get out of this?"

"Tell them if you want to and tell them it is none of their business if you don't." It was fun to see someone else on the interrogation end after the week she had had.

Freddy sighed. "My dad is a hell-hound."

The guys just blinked in surprise. Benny sipped at her soda, revelling in the sugar and carbonation. She had really missed it.

Smith dived in. "So, are you a hell-hound?"

Benny started snickering, and Freddy kicked her under the table. "Shut up, Benny."

Benny finally decided to pity her friend. "Can I describe it?"

Freddy slumped in relief and nodded.

"She has a canine form with access to the energies of the demon zone. Most of the time, she just reports on sports for the same company I used to write for."

Freddy looked relieved. It was the truth without being the whole truth. It made her other form sound exceptionally impressive, which is why Benny had phrased it that way. Freddy needed more respect than she got.

Benny scooted toward Smith, pressing more firmly against him. "What are the odds of me starting next week?"

He shrugged. "They will probably take a week to work out the paperwork. The mage council has to sign off on your participation as you are a registered mage, not an extranatural."

Tremble chuckled. "Smith is the only one of us who thrives on paperwork. If he says it is so, it is so."

Benny sighed. "It has been a while since I took a week off."

She got up and headed for another round of food. A crowd was starting to gather, and she wanted to fill up before she headed home.

She nodded and held up four fingers when it was her turn at the window. She got a wink and a nod in return as he called the order back in a harsh and guttural tone.

She paid, went to wait with the others and grabbed a handful of sauce packets before she returned to the table, her arms laden with food.

When Benny returned to the table, she had to ask, "So, do you guys normally hang out together, or is this like a time-off thing?"

The agents looked at each other and shrugged.

Tremble said, "We just all wanted tacos tonight, so I called Smith and he got Argyle to drive."

Freddy leaned forward and pointed to Smith, "So, you don't live with your pride." She moved her finger to Argyle,

"You don't live with your master, and you, Tremble, don't live with your clan."

The men all nodded, and Benny wondered where she was going with this.

"So, none of you really have a place in the world, according to your own people." Freddy seemed intent on nailing that down.

Benny whispered, "What are you getting at?"

Her friend snorted. "They have been staring at you like they were hoping that you would put as much enthusiasm into wrapping your mouth around them as you have the tacos. I think I need to know if they can put their focus on you or if they will have split loyalties."

Benny blinked. "Their first loyalty is to the XIA, same as mine will be."

The men looked from one of them to the other. Tremble finally spoke. "Our loyalty is to the XIA, of course."

Argyle leaned in and cleared his

throat. "Though, from what your parents have told us, you might be amenable to having all three of us in a relationship."

Freddy gasped, but Benny cocked her head. "I have considered it, but while it is culturally fine for me and my family wouldn't have an issue with it, I think yours might."

Benny worked on finishing her second order while everyone at the table was in shock. Freddy grabbed one of them, and before Benny could warn her, she bit into it.

Freddy's eyes flared blood red as she fought the heat in her mouth. She gasped and reached for the soda, but Benny shook her head.

"Damn it, what was in there?" Freddy grabbed one of the sodas from the agents and slugged it down.

"Uh, four spicy hot?" Benny felt apologetic.

"And your soda?"

"The same. I needed a bit of a kick today."

The flame in Freddy's eyes faded, and she sat down, eyeing the remaining taco warily. Benny was reaching for it when her phone went off.

She paused. Everyone that would have called her was here at the table. Who the hell could be calling her?

Chapter Three

" $\mathcal{B}$ enny, this is the manor. Please come home." The flat voice of the house she lived in came through the call. The phone was on speaker, and she disconnected the call as it finished speaking.

Benny wadded up her remaining food. "Sorry, folks, I have to go."

Argyle got to his feet, his pale features serious. "We can drive you."

"Pooky will drive me. Freddy, I can drop you on the way home."

"Fuck that, I am coming with you. Get in the car."

The men got up and cleared the table at the same time.

Benny tossed her garbage into the troll-occupied trashcan and headed for the car. The last time she had been called home by the house, one of her school friends had seen her father without his glamour. An investigation had been pending, but her mother passed it off as a demon glamour that she had cast on her husband. It had been a heart-pounding moment.

Pooky opened his door, and she slid into the driver seat. To her shock, Tremble sat in the passenger side. "Freddy is coming with the others."

"Home, Pooky. Quick as you can within legal limits."

The seatbelts snapped into place on both of them, and the car reversed into the lot before taking off on the way home.

"Um, Benny?"

"Yes, Tremble?"

"Who is driving?" He was very polite

about it, but she could tell he was nervous.

"Pooky. He's my car or any other type of conveyance I need. I got him when I was fourteen." She smiled and stroked the dashboard as the car danced with traffic.

"It is enchanted?"

She snickered. "Not specifically. It is a living being that has specific shapeshifting categories. It tends to end up as a vehicle, so Mom and Dad asked if he would be my ride, and he agreed."

"I see. It is an excellent driver."

Benny smiled softly, "He really is. He is also a great designated driver."

"Did I misunderstand earlier, or did you say that you would have a relationship with all three of us?"

Benny blinked at the sudden change of topic. "Um, well, yeah. It wouldn't be right to pick one and leave the other two out of it. So, since you three are partners, I would have to take all three of you on, naturally."

"Some would say there is nothing natural about it. Our species do not blend in nature."

"You work fine in the field. I have seen you three in action. It is a solid balance of teamwork, and I wouldn't put my oar in to knock any of you out. I respect the team, so if I date one, I date the team."

His eyes were wide and his ears were quivering with shock. "That is...that is a very interesting way of thinking of it."

"You have met my parents. I understand that what is required for one relationship is not for another. When you care for someone, you adapt to what they need as long as it doesn't change who you are. You have to know yourself to be able to give that to someone else."

He threaded a hand in her hair and leaned forward. She gave in and kissed him, but when his tongue touched her lips, he jerked back. "What the hell is that?"

She blushed. "Spectre peppers. They were in my soda and my taco. Sorry."

Pooky turned and pulled up to the house, two mage guild cars were parked in the drive. Benny got out of the car the moment that the seatbelt released.

She ran in and yelled at the mages who were firing spells at the library. "Hey!"

The spellcasters paused.

A woman with dark hair asked, "Do you live here?"

"Yes. What is the issue?" Benny asked.

"There is a demon on the premises, and we have to take him into custody."

"May I look?" There was no reason not to ask to see what they were trying to pry out of the library. It might actually be a demon.

"Be careful, miss."

Benny glanced over, and her friends were arriving. "They are with me. I was out when I got the call."

She stepped into the group of mages and looked into the library. Her mother and father were floating in the air, and between them was an actual demon—Yomra the demon high king, her great-great grandfather.

Huge antlers sprung from his head, his clawed hands and dark-blue skin gleamed wetly; the spikes down his back were almost as intimidating as the club between his legs.

An oily voice in her mind knocked her to her knees. *Ah, little Beneficia, just as lovely as Kyria with far less wear and tear. I will strike a deal with you. Your parents can return to their lives if you agree to come and work for me. I think you would make an excellent succubus.*

The distended erection he sported

made her gag. Benny shook her head. *No. I will not work for you, but I will come for them.*

I give you a week to change your mind, pet. You will be mine. If you don't come to me, I will call you by blood and that is not going to be a comfortable moment for you. Remember, it is my blood in your veins. I own it, and I will own you.

A thunderclap of power and they were gone.

Benny was still on the floor, and the moment the pressure on her mind disappeared, she fainted.

Waking with her friends around her confused her; it took her seconds before she realised what had just happened. "He took them."

Freddy nodded. "That is what the mages say. They are waiting to interview you. I am guessing that they are pissing themselves at having seen an actual demon for the first time in their lives."

Smith leaned forward. "Why did he take them?"

She cast a silencing spell on the area around them and whispered, "He wants me. He wants me to take over for Kyria. If I don't agree, he will pull me in by blood and that won't be good for me."

Tremble took her hand. "What does that mean?"

"Blood call will take my free will and imprison my soul. You can't normally have a soul and be summoned by blood, but if anyone could find a way, he would." She shivered. "My brain still feels oily."

A thud on her silence spell told her they weren't alone anymore. She dismissed the spell, and the four mages surged in.

Argyle got to his feet and held up his hand. "Our teammate has just had a nasty shock. Not only were her parents kidnapped, but there were mages in her home."

The woman that had first spoken smiled, "I am Agent Wells. I need to ask you some questions about the intruder."

"Do you have access to the records of the Ganger family? The recent ones?"

Agent Wells looked uncomfortable discussing it in mixed company. "Yes, there is some demon in the bloodline?"

"That demon is where the blood originated. His name is Yomra. He has kidnapped my parents."

"Do you know why?"

"Because he is a fucking demon. He was a contributing factor in the women who were murdered two weeks ago. These officers of the XIA stopped those plans." She gestured to the men around her.

Freddy smiled and waved.

"Ah, and Freddy is my best friend.

She is familiar with my family dynamic."

Freddy nodded, "I have known the Gangers for years. They are good citizens, excellent teachers and Lenora is a great cook."

"Why would he come to you?"

Benny sighed. "Blood binding. He can do a lot with the blood of two of the strongest mages of our current age. Either I turn my blood over or he will capture me and hurt my parents."

"Why not just take you?"

Argyle snorted. "Blood taken from the unwilling loses power. It can still be useful for a purpose, but you cannot build on its strength. He needs her cooperation."

That he was supporting her in her lie was a relief. She tried to look pale and shaken. It wasn't too difficult.

Agent Wells stared at her, but nodded. "You have had a rough time. We will begin negotiations with the demon zone and see what we can find out. I am afraid that your father's bloodline might make that awkward for him, but your mother should be fine."

"Thank you, Agent Wells. I will be here or you can get me through the XIA. I have just been cleared to be mage liaison for this XIA team."

Her chair shifted, and to her shock, she was sitting on Smith's lap. No wonder she had been so comfortable.

Benny looked up at him, and he smiled down at her, looping his arms around her waist. It wasn't the most professional appearance, but it made Agent Wells uncomfortable enough to quickly take down her contact information before mentioning that there would be a car out front until they had answers about the origin of the demon.

Benny asked a question. "How did you find out about the demon?"

Agent Wells flicked through her

notes. "Someone named Manor called it in."

Benny nodded. With the suspension spell, it would have had to have been the house itself. "Thanks."

"Do you know Manor?"

"I do. He lives in the area." She suddenly had a thought. "Jessamine!"

Benny jumped out of Smith's lap and ran for the alcove where Jessamine's remains were stored. Benny opened the box and sighed with relief. In a tiny portrait, her friend and housemate was sobbing softly, claw marks and blood stained her clothing, but she was still in one piece. "Jess. Oh thank goodness."

Jess looked up and sobbed with relief. "Oh, Benny. He was here and through the wards in no time. He used some of Kyria's blood to break in."

"Do you need help?"

"Please."

Benny whispered a spell to heal ectoplasm and watched the claw marks fade. Jessamine manifested near her, and she looked devastated.

"I couldn't do anything."

"Mom and Dad couldn't either. Don't worry about it. We are going to get through this."

Agent Wells was staring in shock. "You have a ghost?"

Jessamine stiffened and floated up to the woman. "Hey, Benny, you have an idiot?"

Benny snorted. "Jessamine was a friend of the family a few centuries ago. She is now a companion and my room-mate. I normally live at the dower house at the end of the lane, but my parents are doing renovations, so I am staying at the manor until the renos are done."

Agent Wells nodded. "Well, I have your information, so I will be on my way. Take this and keep it on you in case you need anything."

Benny took the card the woman handed her, ignoring the zing of tracking magic embedded in it.

When the mages were gone, her ghost was back, the agents were staring at her and Freddy was eating cookies. Benny got ready to go and rescue her parents from the demon zone.

Chapter Four

$\mathcal{B}$enny took a deep breath and muttered, "Just like Easter."

Freddy explained the comment to the men. "She means it is time to make a battle plan."

She walked to the library, put her hands on either side of the doorway and sent a cleaning spell through it to remove every trace of blood. When the nine popping flames finally confirmed that she had found them all, she mentally cursed her great grandmother and headed into the best magical library for several hundred miles.

"You might want to keep your heads down." She called out the warning before she set up a summoning spell. The spell was specific. She wanted a way to expunge the link to the living demon in her bloodline. With her growing power, there was no way that Yomra wasn't going to try to get his hands on her, now that he was aware of her.

Books flew toward her, and she caught them, stacking them on the table one by one. The books would get her close, but she might have to get help.

"Can any of you read spell books?"

Her four companions shook their heads.

Benny fished her phone out of her pocket and flipped through her contacts. She hoped it wasn't too early.

The phone rang three times before a scratchy voice answered. "Hello?"

"Minerva?"

"Yes. Is this Benny?"

Benny sighed with relief. "Yes. I need help."

"What do you need?"

"You. I need someone who can read spells and intuit a new option."

"At your place or the manor?"

"The manor."

"I am on my way."

Benny felt tears running down her cheeks. "Thank you. You don't know how much this means to me."

"No problem. Now, let me hang up so I can get dressed. I will be there in five."

Benny nodded but the call was over. She put her phone back in her pocket and smiled. "You guys don't have to hang around. I am going to get going on this today."

Freddy snorted. "Right. I will make some coffee; you start whatever you were going to do."

Benny kept a polite smile on her face while Freddy headed into the kitchen. She grabbed Smith's arm. "Do *not* let her make the coffee unless you want to be able to see into next week."

He nodded and went to rescue the coffee.

"Argyle, we keep a guest room upstairs with no windows if you want to lie down for a while."

Argyle came up to her and kissed her softly. "We will get your parents back."

She stroked the blood-red silk of his hair. "I know, I just want to do it before Yomra hurts them. Demons are not known for their self-control."

Her eye was glowing. She could see it when Argyle headed up the stairs and Tremble walked up to her. It glowed against his skin, and she felt the silk of his hair against her face when he kissed her.

She wanted to curl up in his arms and sob, but this wasn't the time. Just outside the manor, she felt Minerva's arrival. "She's arrived. I have to let her in."

Benny made her way to the door and

opened it before the agents outside could notice the mage in the archway. Minerva was standing on the steps with a bandolier of tubes and vials around her and two large bags over her shoulders. "Let's figure this out."

Benny hugged her and invited her inside.

Minerva stepped in and her breathing was a little shallow.

"There are three XIA agents here and Freddy. They are making coffee and biscuits to keep us up and running."

"Thanks, it takes a lot of effort to maintain this figure." Minerva quirked her lips.

Minerva was plus sized in all the right places. She was nearly six feet tall, had wicked curves and a lush body that made other women envious, though she would never see it. Minerva was used to being an amazon amongst Victorian ladies. She was designed for battle and had no idea how lovely she truly was.

Minerva rubbed her hands together. "What do you need and where do you want me to start?"

Benny drew her friend into the library, and she walked over to the tomes that her spell had pulled out.

"Minerva, I need your help to locate or create a spell that can cut the ties between a demon and his children."

Her friend whistled long and low. The magic in the sound vibrated in the air. "That is quite the complicated arrangement. Why are we doing this?"

Benny sat and looked up at her with her exhaustion showing in her body. "My great-great grandfather took my father and mother and is holding them hostage for my cooperation as his newest succubus."

Minerva's lip curled. "That is revolting."

"I just want to get my parents back

here and keep Yomra from pulling the whole blood-link thing. To do that, we need to find a way to break the connection that all demons share with their sire."

Minerva tapped her lips. "Maybe not all demons. Is your family a straight line?"

"Pretty much. One child to one child and so on."

Minerva grinned. "Excellent. I think I know of a way to do this."

"I summoned all the books that might have a base spell to what we need."

Minerva gestured to the table and the near dozen tomes stacked up. "Can I get started?"

"You can."

"Go and get some rest, Benny. I will have one of your crew call you if I find anything." Minerva cracked the first book open and settled at the table, flipping quickly with her eyes glowing bright.

Mage sight was a rare gift, and it was one of a dozen or more that Minerva possessed. Benny got to her feet, wavered and smiled at her friend. "Anything at all, get them to call me."

"Go. Sleep. I will keep you posted."

Benny nodded and put her hand on Minerva's shoulder. "Thanks, Minerva."

"Anytime. It is the Mage Guide oath."

Benny chuckled. "Right up there with the defence of chocolate act."

"You've got it. Now go. I got this."

It was a dismissal given with a pat on her hand before Minerva shifted her focus back to the tome in front of her.

Benny headed out of the library and toward the stairs. To her surprise, Tremble followed her from his post in the doorway.

"What are you doing?"

"Benny, you are in danger, and we are fully trained to help with your situation.

You are going to be guarded until you are no longer in jeopardy. That includes when you sleep."

Since he wasn't on duty, his hair was hanging loose, and as she glanced back at him, the curtain swung and caught the light. *Damn, he's pretty.*

She passed the blackout room and the door was open a crack, letting her see that Argyle was on the bed and watching television.

He called out, "Come on in."

Benny looked back at Tremble, and he shrugged that he didn't mind.

She walked into the dimness and looked at the vampire wearing nothing but his shorts and a sheet. "I have been ordered to nap."

"I am willing to share space if you are. Even the big fairy can come on in."

Benny yawned and kicked her shoes off, skinning out of her jeans, tossing her shirt and unsnapping her bra.

Argyle was staring at her, and Tremble was draped in her tank top. With another yawn, she climbed onto the bed and yanked the sheets up around her.

"You are very nonchalant about sharing the bed with two men."

Benny sighed. "My parents have been kidnapped by a demon who wants me to screw mages for a living, so being in bed with two men I can trust is definitely something I want to enjoy while I can."

Argyle scooted down in the bed and pulled her against him, rubbing her back. Tremble joined them, and with her body protected front and back, she slept.

Benny felt the change in the energy of the room, and she sat up, staring at Jessamine. The ghost was waving at her, and Benny slipped out from between the two men. Argyle was in his restorative state, and Tremble was just snoring lightly.

Benny pulled her shirt on and slipped into her jeans, tiptoeing out of the room and down to the library.

Minerva was scribbling in a twenty-five-cent notebook. She had a cup of coffee next to her and a small stack of crescent rolls.

When Benny followed Jessamine into the room, Minerva looked up and smiled with her eyes glowing brightly. "I think I have it. You are going to need some very specific things, and they will not be easy to acquire, but the magic is sound."

"You think?"

Minerva stretched, her ink-stained fingers reached for the sky. "Pretty sure."

"How sure?"

"If I help you...about ninety-three percent sure." She smiled. "The next full moon is Wednesday, so we are going to have to do it by then."

Benny felt a chill in her stomach.

"Why the time constraint?"

"I have a date to act as a proxy in a negotiation with a dragon. I have to be in Sumac Heart City by the full moon."

Benny sat down and put her head in her hands. "Okay. Tell me what we need."

"Well, knowing your mother, we have access to the first two dozen ingredients. The unicorn horn and dragon skin will be tricky."

Benny shook her head. "We have some. Show me the list."

Minerva quickly jotted down the list and divided it into animal and herbal matter. "Here you go. I have the ones I ticked off here." She pointed to a pile of herbs and vials in the centre of the table.

"Are the quantities enough?"

"Oh yeah. Most of this only requires a token of the herb to act as a focus. As you know, my magic focuses on intent, not in strong arming the result."

"It's why you were the first person I thought of. Thank you so much for helping."

"It is fine. I love a good puzzle, and I love your parents. They were the first folks to not bat an eye at my growth spurt. Your mom just gave me an extra serving of everything." Minerva's eyes got a little misty as she smiled at the memory.

Benny put her hand on Minerva's arm. She rested her head on her friend's shoulder. Minerva had gone from the smallest in the class to the tallest in the class in the course of eighteen months. Her body had been wracked with pain, and she ate constantly. Minerva's mother had come to Benny's in search of help for her daughter. Lenora had worked up a daily dose that would help Minerva's body grow to its full potential. No one had any idea that there was any extranatural in the bloodline until she finished growing.

"Well, Benny, if you are up for it, let's go into the greenhouse and pick out what we need from your mother's stores."

Benny nodded, looked down and made a face. "Let me change."

She cast a quick spell and cleaned herself up as well as put on a bra and new shirt from her room.

Smith came in with Freddy, and they paused. "Benny, you look..."

Freddy winced. "Eyes, Benny."

With a deep breath, she pushed her demon back inside and brushed her hands on her thighs. "Better?"

Smith nodded. "Better. Where are the others?"

"Argyle is restoring himself and Tremble is snoring. I snuck out while they were unconscious."

Smith scowled. "You were in bed with both of them?"

Minerva blushed and cleared her throat. "I will be waiting outside the greenhouse."

Freddy grinned. "Come on, Benny, tell all."

"Argyle feels like cool sheets, and Tremble starts as a snuggler who rolls to his back the moment he is out. All we did was sleep. Tremble wanted to start something, but even he wouldn't make a move in front of Argyle." She sighed and patted Smith on the cheek. "We slept. I needed it."

He pressed his forehead to hers and inhaled. "Fair enough."

"You just sniffed me to see if I had had sex with your partners." She whispered it against his cheek.

"Yes. You didn't." He sighed. "How is this going to work?"

"We are going to take turns. I will be with you, with them, and I promise to keep all things equal while we are together." She smiled and patted his shoulder.

"Seriously? All of us?" He looked so hopeful.

She sighed. "Not at the same time, but yes. I don't play favourites, and as Freddy can tell you, I have a knack for knowing what I need. I need all of you."

Freddy's hand was over her mouth, but she nodded and mumbled, "She does know what she needs."

Benny stroked his cheek and gave him a quick peck. "I will see you later. Now, we have to get my parents back. You go for a nap and I will be with Minerva. Freddy can watch me. She doesn't need sleep."

Freddy saluted sharply. "I have this covered, Smith. Get going. There are a dozen rooms upstairs. Take one and sleep. We need to be at our best."

Benny smiled softly as Smith headed up the stairs. "Speaking of being at our best. Thanks for staying for this, Freddy."

"No problem. I know where this is taking us, and I am with you all the way."

Benny teared up as they headed to the greenhouse. It wasn't every friend that would follow you into the demon zone.

Chapter Five

Minerva was wisely waiting and re-arranging her lists. No one wanted to go into Lenora's greenhouse if they didn't know what they were looking for.

Benny grabbed the handles on the doors and felt the magic of the house recognize her. She opened the greenhouse, and Minerva followed her.

Freddy waved, "I am going to wait out here."

Benny gave her a thumbs-up and led Minerva through the temperature lock before opening the inner doors. "Remember. Elbows in and let me know if anything grabs you."

"Yes, ma'am. You want the list?"

"Yup. You take the basket." Benny reached over and took her mother's collection basket.

Minerva clutched the woven bark with both arms and followed faithfully in Benny's footsteps.

Benny looked down at the list, and they started shopping.

Snipping carefully to take only what she needed, Benny followed the recipe to a tee. "What the heck are tears of the gorgon?"

"Rocks. Tiny pieces of marble. Your mom has them in the lab."

"Why don't you just say marble chips?"

"Because it doesn't sound fancy." Minerva chuckled. "No, they are really tears of a gorgon. Their transformation and ability to transform others makes them weep for the first two weeks during their adulthood. Their tears are those of a lost past and a fixed future alone."

Benny paused. "That is so sad."

"That is why they cry. It plays the part of finality in the spell and mourns the loss of the past even if you do not feel regret."

It made sense, and Benny clipped the last clinging vine that she needed. It writhed disturbingly in the bottom of the basket.

"We are good. Everything else is a in the dry-storage cupboard in the lab."

Minerva nodded, her elbows carefully tucked in. "You go first."

Benny chuckled and headed for the entrance, past the deadly plants that Minerva found so unsettling. She extended her personal aura, and the plants drew back, giving them a wide berth while they exited the greenhouse.

Minerva was right behind her when Benny opened the temperature lock. Her friend sighed with relief when they were out in the hall and on the way to the lab.

Benny remembered weekends with Minerva, sitting on a stool while her friend and her mother were lost in their herbs and powdered whatsits. She had sat and looked over cupcake recipes while Minerva learned what Benny took for granted—the mechanics of magic.

The lab was far less dangerous to walk through, but Benny still moved carefully. She checked the recipe and got the burner and the bowl made of raw iron.

Minerva found the cutting board, and she carefully picked her knife. Without speaking, she got to work.

Benny got the rest of the immediate ingredients together and stood near Minerva. "What should I be doing?"

"Make a binding spell. You can't go in alone, but I can't track anyone but you when you enter the zone."

"I will have Freddy with me."

"You will need more. Freddy is great,

but she can be controlled by a demon king."

Freddy poked her head in. "She isn't wrong."

Benny chuckled, but then she sighed. "I don't want to haul anyone into my mess."

Freddy snickered, "The boys are coming along. You don't even have to ask. As soon as I explained what you were going to be up against, Smith told me they were in. Make the binding potion."

Minerva chuckled. "It will give you something to do and keep you occupied until your sleeping beauties wake up. If you don't use it, you only waste time and a few ingredients."

Benny sighed and went to the recipe book on the wall, hauling it down and flipping through the pages. "Fine."

She got to the segment of sharing spells and paused when she saw her father's handwriting correcting one of the lists. She traced the writing and blinked at the date. It was her birthday.

She stared at the notes and confusion ran through her. According to this, she was supposed to be bound to her parents and living grandparents. They were to hold her soul. This was not the spell to shatter her soul and bind her to strangers of the same age; it wasn't even close.

Benny flipped through the pages and a folded sheet fell out. She read the notes and tears rushed to her eyes. She breathed in through her nose and out through her mouth, controlling her emotions until she could continue looking for the binding spell she needed. She carefully tucked the small note back where she found it. It wasn't for her; it was a note for her father. She had never realised that this book was his.

Minerva glanced at her. "Is something wrong?"

"No, I just never realised that my father had been the primary herbalist until he changed. Mom had been into the raw-energy spellcasting and natural magic."

Minerva paused with her pestle raised. "I didn't know that."

Freddy piped in. "It makes sense. Demon magic makes it hard to concentrate on things like time-consuming herbals and spells. They are much more instinctive and aggressive when it comes to magic."

Benny nodded, that described what her father had been doing since she was ten. She found the recipe she needed and checked the basket. All the herbs were out of it. "Can I take the basket?"

"Please. I have taken every crumb."

Benny grabbed the basket and headed back into her own private jungle. She inhaled the bright, rich scents of the herbs essential to spellcasting. For this spell, she needed vines and plants with sticky sap. She took the special non-stick blades out of their drawer and got to work.

The sap leaves had to be lined up just so in the basket or they would dribble their contents everywhere. The creeping vines that tried to hang onto her were a hazard to the balance in the basket, so she had to keep an eye on them.

When she returned to the lab, she felt like she had her mother with her. She got herself a wooden bowl bound with silver and got to work. First, the vines went in and the sap was poured over top. She got a crystal pestle and went to work.

Since it was binding for tracking, she added a werewolf's claw and the mucus of a snail for a trail. The other ingredients were ground into the sap, and then, it was time to put magic in it.

Freddy perked up, this was her favourite part. Benny smiled, put her hands over the bowl and pulled magic out of her to transform the contents. Benny opted for orange-soda flavour.

"There. All done but the blood."

Minerva was still grinding away, sweat on her brow. "Good. Go and drop it in."

Benny shook her head. "Nope. This is a four-way binding spell. It will attach me to them and them to me, as well as each other. I am going to have to make damned sure that they want that or this is going nowhere."

"Why didn't you use a standard spell?"

"Because this has to be equal all the way around or nothing. My binding them to me would be selfish in the extreme."

Minerva shook her head. "It isn't selfish, it is destiny. You have always known what you needed in life, and whom you needed around you. That is some of your fey blood. You must have a seer on your mother's side somewhere."

Benny used a funnel to get the binding potion into a flask. It was glass bound with silver and had the engraving of her mother's and father's initials. It was a wedding gift, and she felt it was appropriate to use it for this particular potion.

Minerva whistled softly. "Is that an Eckerhart?"

"I don't know. It has always been around, and my mom told me it was only for potions that revolved around the family. This definitely counts."

Minerva rummaged through the vials on the bandolier and brought out a small gold capsule. "Add all of this to the binding spell. You need it there more than I do on the outside."

Benny took the small, engraved capsule with reverence. She pried open the vial and sniffed. Wild green, open air, a love song in the distance and the battering of the ocean against rocks. "What is it?"

"Luck. The luck of life. One thousand shamrocks distilled in the bright sunlight and ground with the purest salt from the sea. One grain is enough for a normal being to bless them for a lifetime. You are going to need it."

Benny tapped the crystals out of the vial one at a time until all twenty-three had spilled into the orange, swirling liquid, and it changed to silver with flecks of gold.

She made sure that the gold vial was empty, and she pressed it back into Minerva's hand. "Thank you."

"You are welcome. It needs to be shared, and I can't think of anyone more deserving than you of some bright, new luck."

Freddy looked up, "What about me?"

Benny chuckled. "You will be with me, and your summoner is not in the zone right now."

Freddy perked up. "You know that?"

"I always keep tabs on her. I know where she is every moment of every day. Right now, she is across the world." Benny patted her friend on the shoulder, rubbing in the small crystal of luck she had kept behind.

Freddy blinked, and her eyes flared red for a moment. She nodded and smiled. "Good. The less I hear from her, the better."

Being bound to a mage came with being a hellhound. When Freddy was born, across the world, her mage came into the world. They met when the mage was a teenager, and she chose Freddy's form. The first summoning had pulled Freddy out of the mall and across the globe. When the need was over, Freddy was back in the seat she had been taken from, in the lap of the new occupant. Freddy was stuck with the hound first chosen. The form was set and the connection was made.

Benny might be bound to her family, but Freddy was bound to a stranger who never took her wellbeing into account. It was all about what her mage wanted and the hound was never consulted.

She corked the flask and looked at the silver and gold swirl. "I really hope this works."

The sound of approaching footsteps brought the Y-chromosome into the room in the form of Argyle and Tremble. Smith stumbled in a moment later, rubbing his eyes and looking delightfully sexy.

Argyle asked, "Why are all the ladies in here?"

Minerva chuckled. "We are cooking...sort of. Can you guys go and fix dinner? We have been working all day."

Smith nodded and saluted her. "Yes, ma'am."

The three agents filed out of the lab and clanging could be heard in the kitchen.

Benny cleaned up her workstation and sent all the residue of the spell into the catch basin under the house. Everything was scrubbed and put back where it was supposed to be.

Minerva was still working on her spell, but based on the steam bubbling up from the vessel, it was nearly complete.

Benny asked, "Do you want me to keep you company?"

Minerva shook her head. "Nope. Go on and keep an eye on your men. You can explain the binding spell to them using the paper cup and straws analogy."

"Yes, ma'am." Benny bowed and took the flask.

Freddy piped up, "I will keep her company."

Minerva grinned. "Bring in dinner. I still have an hour to go."

"Yay and yes." Benny gave her a thumbs-up and went to rescue her kitchen. It sounded like it was in distress.

Chapter Six

The surprisingly graceful ballet of chopping, mixing and flipping was taking place in her kitchen.

She was surprised that Argyle was involved, but he was boiling pasta with an eye for it approaching the precise doneness.

Tremble glanced over his shoulder. "What were you working on?"

"Minerva is getting a spell ready to sever the family connections with a demon. I was working on a binding spell in case anyone wants to come with me." She put that out in the open.

Three men turned to her, but Argyle turned the stove down first. The vampire crossed his arms. "Of course we are coming with you. You are not going into the demon zone alone."

She cocked her head. "It isn't that easy. To get into the zone, you need demon blood. To get that blood, you need to have it in you and bound to you. It would contaminate your bloodlines, possibly permanently."

"What would we be bound to?" Tremble cocked his head.

"Me. Well, not just me, but to each other. It would be an equivalent sharing of power and awareness with everyone involved in the spell. So, whoever were involved would be bound together, not just by demon blood, but by whatever was in the mix."

Tremble picked up on the ramifications. "So, I would have links to vampire, shifter and demon?"

"As well as the fey and mage bloodlines I bring to the mix."

They paused together. Benny smirked. "Do you want to discuss it without me here?"

Tremble shook his head. "No. We are coming with you, and if the binding spell is what it takes, then we are willing to bind to you and each other."

Argyle and Smith nodded.

Argyle said, "I am good with it."

Smith grinned, "My mom will be so impressed."

She laughed. "Well, did you want to do this before dinner or after?"

Tremble asked, "What do you need us to do?"

"Four drops of blood into the flask, drawn with a knife. No teeth. You don't want saliva getting in here." She patted the flask.

Smith went to the cutlery drawer and pulled out four steak knives before handing them out.

Everyone gathered around the kitchen island, and she opened the flask. With a quick motion, she stabbed her pinky and dropped the knife, squeezing four drops out without difficulty.

Argyle went next. It took him a while to get the vampire blood to drip, but after a minute, he finished.

Smith was quick, and Tremble's blood looked like it was loaded with glitter.

Benny corked the flask and tipped it to get the blood drops from the sides. The liquid turned to a molten bronze; four cups appeared on a chain around the flask.

"That is different. Well, here goes."

She unhooked the cups and lined them up, pouring an equal measure of the spell into each vessel. She set the flask down and lifted her cup to the men standing with her. They each picked up a cup, and all of them brought the cups together.

"Let's hope this works. I am a little

rusty on my potion making."

Benny brought her cup to her lips, and the orange was still there, along with the wild taste of the luck and the pungent flavour of blood. She drained the cup. The power hit her a moment later.

Benny slammed her hands down to the table, watching as her skin changed shape, texture and claws appeared and disappeared. The other three were in the same condition. Ears pointed and reset, eyes flicked and skins changed colour.

It took several minutes, and they were all covered with sweat when the magic had linked them from the inside out.

Smith shook his head. "That was...wow."

Argyle looked at his hands. "My heart started beating for a moment."

Tremble was blinking rapidly. "I felt so much."

Benny took a deep breath. "You will

be able to access the power of the others as needed, even my power, though you guys don't have the training to work the human magic."

Smith looked at her. "Why do I feel like I can bench press a cow?"

Benny pointed at Argyle. "That comes from him. You will all experience flashes of instincts that belong to the others. That is normal."

Tremble focused. "What about you; won't you experience a change?"

She shrugged. "I already have all three of your races in my bloodline. I deal with all of those instincts every day. What you need to watch out for is the trickle of demon blood. If one of you asserts that, they can take control; the others need to smack him. The constant urge to dominate others with aggression is one of the signs. Enforcing your will with levitated objects is another."

Smith looked at her with narrowed

eyes. "You would not have handed un-controllable power to us."

"You are right. I can pull you back if I need to, but it sounds a little bossy." She shrugged.

Tremble blinked, rubbed his eyes and blinked again. "I keep seeing a face over-lapping yours."

"The demon blood gives you another presence, and if it is strong enough, another form completely. You will see me wearing that other form when we go to the demon zone. I won't have a choice. The magic that binds the demons into the zone keeps human enchantments from being effective. We will have our bodies and our wits. That is it."

Argyle tilted his head. "What about weapons?"

Benny shook her head. "No. I will explain the details later. Finish cooking, Minerva is going to need her strength."

As if her words released them, they

turned and resumed cooking. Benny sighed and took the flask back to the lab for cleaning.

Minerva was putting the salve she had created into a glass jar. "Got it. Just two more ingredients and the spell will be complete."

"And that is blood from Yomra and blood from me."

"Right. It will sever the link between you and ripple down all layers of your family. You will still be of the demon breed, but you will be free."

Benny nodded. "Slice through the demon magic that binds me and Yomra can't call on my family."

"Even Kyria will be loose. Sorry, but Freddy filled me in." Minerva got every drop of the salve into the jar, sealed it, and then, she carefully took the empty raw-iron bowl to the sink and poured in nullifier. Bright sparks flew, and Minerva quickly cleaned out the vessel before drying it and heating it on the small burner once again.

While Minerva worked, Benny used the nullifier in the flask and swished it out before dumping the potion into the sink with the catch basin. After that, she was free to use water.

When it was clean and dry, she set the flask back on the shelf and closed the glass-paned door.

The smells coming from the kitchen were delightful, and with the salve ready, the spell-casting implements washed and a strong hunger, they all trooped out of the lab and into the kitchen. There was just something about pasta when you needed to fill up and prepare to break part of your family tree into a pile of splinters.

Benny watched Argyle when the rest of them started eating. When she took her first bite, his eyes widened and he swallowed. She grinned, and he looked at her in surprise.

"I can taste it. I used too much oregano."

She chuckled and swallowed. "Focus on one of the others."

Tremble drank some wine, and Argyle's eyes fluttered and his lips pressed together.

"Holy..." He smiled as his words trailed off. His fangs were on display while he spoke, and he closed his eyes to savour it.

Tremble blinked. "He is tasting what I eat?"

Benny chuckled. "Of course. We are bound." She smirked. "It works with sex as well if you were wondering."

Minerva coughed wildly. Freddy patted her on the back, but her own cheeks were on fire.

Argyle was grinning and Tremble finally caught on.

"So, that is why you said that being with all three of us wouldn't be a problem. What one feels, the others feel."

Benny kept eating and mumbled, "Only when you concentrate."

Minerva sighed. "Didn't you explain it to them?"

Benny grinned. "Not really."

Minerva took a mouthful of food and got to her feet. She went to the cupboard and got four paper cups and a handful of straws that she snipped in two. "Benny's blood is symbolized by the water in this cup. She could give you each some..." Minerva poured a splash of water into each cup.

"If she did that, the blood would not have a connection to her, and after a while, you would consume it, or it would evaporate."

Minerva set the four cups out, and with a touch of magic, she dyed each one a different colour. "These are all of you, each a different power. If we connect them with the binding spell..." She waved her fingers and the straws bridged around in a spoke pattern and then connections for the agents' cups.

"The powers are stable unless someone injures one of them." Minerva took an ice cube out of her glass, and she dropped it in the *Benny* cup. The colour moved out of the cup through the straws. "She then gets strength from each of you and you get strength from each other. Usually, it is only done between a maximum of three people, but this one seems to be working quite well."

Minerva waved at the cups, and they floated up and into the sink. "The point of that spell is to keep you equal at all times. Your magic will still be separate for the most part, but it will flow when it needs to."

Benny finished her meal and got up to start the dishes. She scrubbed and smiled as she heard Argyle discussing how food actually tasted. Apparently, he had been craving the taste of food since she let him taste his first taco through her veins.

She blinked away tears. It seemed like so long ago, but it had been less than a month since her world had spun out of her control. So many firsts in that time, and now, her parents were in danger because of her. Her stomach flipped at the thought of what she was about to do. It was only in the security of her home that she had discussed the demon zone. Even her father had never set foot in the place.

Dishes and cutlery started to appear on her left, and she washed, rinsed and set the dishes on the draining board in rapid succession.

"How much time has passed, Freddy?"

"Seventeen hours, Benny. You will

have most of the night in the zone."

Benny nodded and dried her hands. "I need to get the map. Someone else can dry the dishes."

Freddy nodded. "I will. I know you hate doing it."

Benny wanted a moment alone. She needed to talk to the house.

She left the group in the kitchen with a tight smile and headed for the library, closing the door behind her.

"Hello, house."

The phone rang.

Smiling, Benny went to pick up the receiver. "Hello, house."

"Hello, Benny."

"You know what I am about to do?"

"It is very dangerous." The calm, masculine tone spoke the truth.

"If we do not return, I want you to welcome Minerva as your new occupant. She will respect you and all that is within you."

"You will return."

"I hope I will, and Mom and Dad too, but I am bracing for the possibility that we will not. I want you taken care of in a manner that you deserve. Minerva knows you. She will respect you and listen to your council."

"I will accept her if the Gangers do not return." The voice was resigned.

There was a moment of silence before he said, "There is a present for you on the desk. I have enjoyed watching you grow, and you deserve the protection that I can offer."

Benny looked around and found a box that gleamed with a black silk ribbon. "Do I open it now?"

"You will need it where you are going. Demon eyes cannot see it. Wear it and be safe." The line went dead.

She put the handset down on the phone and tugged the ribbon loose. She opened the ten-inch box, and tears pricked her eyes again. A knife made of ebony and obsidian was nestled in the box next to a sheath with thigh straps.

She slid the blade into the sheath and looked at it, flicking to her demon vision. She could still feel it, but it was invisible. Grinning, she flicked back to normal vision and strapped it to her left thigh.

Humming to herself, she got the map and flicked her hand to open the library doors. They swung open, and her entourage stumbled inside.

The map was gross, but keeping an interdimensional diagram on normal parchment wasn't possible. A gargoyle's wing hosted the map, and since it did not dry out, the map was rather lifelike.

She pinned the wing open and whispered over the skin in a language that had no name, but haunted the nightmares of anyone who heard their name spoken in it.

The zone took shape and projected into a three-dimensional drawing of the home of the demons. She whispered, "Yomra."

A light glowed in the centre of the city.

"Harcourt Emile Ganger." A blue light lit in the same building as the yellow.

"Agatha Lenora Ganger." A purple light glowed near the blue one. It was a relief.

"Kyria." Hot pink burned a few buildings away. That was something. At least she wasn't going to have to contend with a demon high king and her great grandmother.

She memorized the map and smiled tightly. "Minerva, do you have a few extra vials?"

Minerva smiled. "Always." She fished a few vials out of her bag and held them out. "They have magnetic flip tops. No magic involved."

Benny carefully arranged the vials around her body, each with the top wedged open. If she had to get close enough to get Yomra's blood, she was going to make damned sure she collected it.

Chapter Seven

Pooky transformed into a van when they left the house. They were all silent as the car drove to the Redbird City Park.

Minerva made a few phone calls during the drive. She was the only one who was going to be alone during the procedure, and they were depending on her to get them out. She called on a few friends of hers to come and watch her back while she worked on keeping them safe, even from a distance.

Benny looked at Minerva as she dialled yet another friend. "I wish I could help you with this."

"This is out of your territory. I need

folks who will blend in but have my back. Your friends are not known for blending in." Minerva smirked. "I can call in a few favours."

Smith asked, "How are you going to get us out?"

Minerva put her phone to her ear. "I am going to keep my foot in the door."

She continued calling until they arrived at the park.

Benny parked and asked for a moment alone. When she was with Pooky, she asked him for the same favour that she had the house. To her surprise, Pooky refused.

"Fine, if I do not return, run wild and free until you choose to drive around with another teenager." She chuckled and stroked the dashboard. "It has been an honour to be with you."

He rumbled the engine.

What he was saying was clear. He had enjoyed himself as well.

She stroked the steering wheel. "I hope to see you again in a few hours."

The engine purred and the door opened.

She got out and headed toward her group.

Minerva made a glowing orb, and she had a selection of vials and a folded piece of cloth. Minerva held them out toward her. "The cloth will open all doors. It is a piece of the gown of Giltine, but it can also summon sudden death."

"I know who she is. Thank you." Benny smiled tightly and put the cloth in a pocket of the courier bag she had across her body.

"These are healing potions. They won't do you a lot of good in the zone, but you can take them the moment I grab you, and they will start working when you hit the threshold."

Benny nodded and stuffed them into her bra and pockets. Her clothing would transform along with everything else, so it was best to keep things as close to the skin as she could.

She checked the height of the moon in the sky and beckoned to Freddy. "If you still want to come, it is show time."

Freddy nodded, her eyes went red and she began to shrink. When she was in her hellhound form, she ran to Benny.

Benny opened the flap of the courier bag, and she scooped the Chihuahua with the glowing red eyes into it. "Thanks, Freddy."

The three XIA agents were staring at the bag and the small head poking out of it. Benny gave them a stern look about ridiculing Freddy for her form.

"Okay, Minerva, can you start?"

Minerva held up her hand as she finished making a glyph in the grass. "And I am ready. Stand on the glyph, and I will wrap you up. Close contact please."

The three men formed an arc, and

Benny nestled in the centre. "Whenever you are ready, Minerva."

The mage smiled and sent out tendrils of light that touched their skin and disappeared with the contact. Benny felt the protective covering going over them, the means by which Minerva would track them. Elementals were funny things, but Minerva had taken to the control that Lenora Ganger had taught her. Benny had known from the moment she met Minerva that the young woman needed to learn from her mother. There had been moments of jealousy, of course, but Benny had gained a friend, and Minerva had gained the tutelage of one of the greatest mages of the age. Everybody came out a winner.

When they were wrapped up with the elemental tags, Minerva lowered her hands. "Okay, I have sparked Benny's blood, so I can find you wherever you are. When you see fire and hear singing, that will be me. Clump together and hold on tight."

Argyle asked, "What if we want early extraction?"

"Benny can manage to get you out. That scrap of fabric will open the wall between dimensions."

Benny put her hand on his arm. "I can also call her or my mother can. You will be out before dawn."

Minerva nodded. "All right. You get going. I will watch the gate."

Benny straightened her shoulders. "Okay, gentlemen. You will be transformed into your demon self. That will include clothing and cell phones. Bear with the changes and walk with me at all times. Our group won't cause much of a stir as long as you guys stay close."

They were with her, step by step, while they approached the gate that she could see clearly.

Smith muttered, "How have I never

seen that before?"

Benny knew he was referring to the electric-blue gateway that they were approaching. "Demon blood is not just for locking folks up. It has a definite positive side, though the lack of a conscience is something you have to get used to working with." She smiled.

One more step and they would be in the gateway. "All right. Everyone put a hand on me."

One hand gripped her left arm, one her right shoulder and two hands gripped her butt. She was so shocked, she took that last step into the gateway and the human world disappeared around them.

Her companions fell to the ground when they entered the demon zone. Benny smiled smugly as she realised that it was where they belonged.

She stretched her arms to the sides,

enjoying the freedom of the leather tabard and belt with thigh-high boots. Her men were wearing rich brown leather that complemented their golden skin, which matched her own.

Benny reached up and touched her horns, smirking at what she discovered. She did not have the stubby horns of her great grandmother or the spikes of her father. She had the majestic horns of a demon high king, and it felt completely right.

Smith got to his feet, a row of short horns running along his skull and his feline features matching his skin tone. He blinked at her, "You look..."

Argyle stood, his pale-gold skin set off by his blood-red hair. He had black sweeping horns that ran along from the front of his skull to the crown where they swept up and away. "She looks splendid."

Tremble spoke from behind her, and

she slowly turned. His skin was a metallic sky blue, and his horns curled on either side of his head in a ram's spiral.

Benny smiled. "You all look splendid as well. Now, please get yourselves together. We have a bit of a walk into the city."

Smith kissed her suddenly, running his hand down her back and cupping her against him. When he released her, she staggered free, and Argyle kissed her, stroking her sides, her butt and generally making free with her.

Argyle was shoved backward when Tremble lifted her off her feet and plastered her against him. After his turn, her blood was pounding in her veins, and it was only her tiny human voice in her mind reminding her that her parents needed her that snapped her out of tackling the boys and rolling around with them for her personal satisfaction.

"Come on. We have to get to Yomra's

palace."

They shook their heads and adjusted their crotches.

Argyle nodded. "I will take point. Let's go."

Benny took Tremble's arm on one side and Smith's on the other. "Let's go."

The city glowed half a kilometre away; it blazed with light. It was very inviting for a den of those who were destined to be painted with the taint of evil, at least as far as humanity was concerned.

As they walked, Tremble asked, "So, how did you end up with those horns?"

She chuckled. "I am descended from royalty. It is more likely than not that I would end up as high king."

She glanced back over her shoulder, and she could see the entryway that Minerva was holding open for them. They just had to find her parents, get some of Yomra's blood and make it back through that door before dawn. *No problem.*

<h1 style="text-align:center">Chapter Eight</h1>

The variety of demons in varying stages of undress was a little startling for her agents, but Benny was used to the sight of demons copulating in the street. Well, she was more used to it happening in the kitchen, but catching your parents doing it for the fiftieth time dulled the shock metre.

She twitched her lips as she watched one acrobatic coupling. "Hey, did anyone end up with a tail?"

Butts were checked and none of her boys had a tail. Too bad. Their leather pants did a lovely job of displaying their assets. Somehow, the magic that had surrounded them on their way in had coordinated their clothing.

Smith asked, "So, demons just have sex out in the open?"

She smiled. "Where would you rather they do it? Behind closed doors and under the sheets? Sex is natural, and they enjoy it when the whim takes them."

She walked with her group through streets that were lined with ancient temples, modern homes and palaces. A few of the demons on the street glanced at them, but once they saw her horns, they quickly looked away and went elsewhere.

The bag with Freddy had turned into a cross-body bag with leather and studwork. Every few blocks, Benny glanced down and met the serious, glowing eyes of the tiny, tiny dog. It kept her from joining any of the groups having sex.

Argyle asked casually, "Is sex the currency here?"

"No. It is the entertainment. They

don't get Wi-Fi or cable, and demons are easily bored."

Tremble muttered, "What about laws?"

"Don't pick a fight with anyone bigger or stronger than you. There is the law of might here. It is really the only law." She smiled.

"So, murder is acceptable here?"

"Acceptable and encouraged. Demons breed when their kings allow, so you want to keep the population in control. The new arrivals are actually protected for a month until they get the hang of it."

Smith murmured, "How do you know so much about it?"

"I have studied the rules of the zone. Knowing that my father could be consigned here at any moment over the last decade and a half meant that I was always interested in it. My grandfather helped me learn."

"How is it that he never changed?"

"He kept his soul, and he never entered the demon zone. My father shared his soul with my mother, so he lost his grip on his human shape." She smiled.

Argyle looked at her with his eyes shadowed. "And he lost his humanity."

She shook her head. "No, he kept it. He has only ever sought my mother for sex in the years since the transformation. As you can see by those we have passed, that is not a usual situation."

There was no doubt about it. While the demons were screwing in public, they were also enticing anyone who passed to join them.

The scent of sex was heavy in the air. Even with the coupling taking place outside, there was still little to no air movement to sweep the pheromones away. Blood was also in the air, but it mixed with the sex in a disturbing way.

Smith looked the most uncomfortable. He was getting the full blast of the scents, and his erection pressed against the leather he was wearing.

She dug her claws into his bicep and whispered the promise, "When we get out of here, I promise to roll around with you until you are exhausted."

He perked up. "Just you and me?"

"Well, Argyle and Tremble can listen in, but yes, just you and me."

He nodded, and it seemed to renew his focus.

The basilica that they were approaching gleamed yellow to her eyes. She nodded with her chin. "That is our destination."

Argyle inclined his head, his crimson hair swinging around him. They walked down the dusty streets until they reached the front entryway of the domed basilica.

"I go first now. Demons like to stab you in the back. I am depending on your three to keep me alive." She smiled for a moment before straightening her features. They were about to face the second most dangerous person in her universe.

Two lesser demons were guarding the entryway.

The green one on the left challenged her. "Why are you here, lady?"

It was nice that her horns at least got her a civil question.

"Lord Yomra has issued an invitation, and I have answered it."

The demon looked at her through evil yellow eyes. "Who are you?"

She straightened and glared at him through her own green eyes. "His blood."

The two guards jerked to full attention. The green one nodded sharply. "Just a moment."

He left his post and entered the building through a small door.

It took three minutes for the large

doors to swing open. She stiffened her shoulders, and she looked at her companions. "Show time."

They nodded with tiny movements of their head, and she could feel that they were prepared to back her up. This entire thing was about her and her family. They were just here for support.

It had to be the roughest first date in history.

The glowing interior cast a weird glow on their skin as they walked into the building and stepped into a throne room, occupied by Yomra himself.

The deep-blue demon got to his feet. "Beneficia! I am delighted to see you, though you are not the demon I had guessed you would be."

"I am consistently full of surprises." She inclined her antlered head.

"You are indeed. Who are your companions?"

"They are mine. Their identities are

no concern of yours."

His serpentine tongue lashed out. "You have invited them into my house."

"They are mine, bound to me." Benny smiled. "They are here to take my parents home."

"Ah, yes. My great grandson and his creature."

Benny stiffened. "That creature is my mother."

"*Was* your mother. She has not been that being for some time." Yomra walked toward her, and she remained in position while he caressed her face with his claws.

He murmured, "Who would have thought that Kyria's spawn would have resulted in this? I should have let her breed more."

He lifted her face to his, and his tongue flicked against her cheek. "You taste of power, little one."

She didn't respond, but she could feel

the agents tense. She sent them a calming wave through the binding. Yomra was merely being a demon.

When he put his lips above hers, she said. "My parents?"

He leaned back, his eyes narrowed. "Why in such a hurry, child?"

"Because they do not belong here."

"He belongs to me, and she does as well, through his blood."

"If I am here, they do not belong here." She remained calm.

He smiled. "I will offer you and your companions dinner while we wait for your parents to be brought to us. Come this way."

He led the way through an archway that appeared as he approached the stone wall. They followed, and the skull-decorated dining hall opened up in front of them.

The polished table was large enough to seat twenty, which amused Benny because demons were not that social.

"Sit at my right hand while I summon your parents."

He lifted his hand, and a ball of power zinged from his palm through the wall.

Benny sat, and she gestured for Tremble to sit at her right hand. Smith and Argyle filed in and sat down. Benny settled Freddy's bag in her lap.

"Your men seem singularly quiet for demons." Yomra looked the agents over.

Benny smiled. "I only met them recently. They are acclimating to the demon energy."

His attention was back on her. "And yet, you got them to bind themselves to you? Well done, child."

The food appeared in the centre of the table. Plates appeared seconds later.

Benny sent a feeling of fullness to her agents. If they ate, it would be harder to pull them free of the zone. The car ride to the park had been full of briefings, but she wanted to remind them. Myths about humans in hell were based on them entering the demon zone and consuming items generated from its power. It was akin to swallowing a battery; if you survived, you had to wait until the effects of the acid wore off.

A doorway opened, and her parents staggered through it. Harcourt and Lenora Ganger looked a little worse for wear, but they were whole.

Benny inclined her head to her father. "Dad, Mom, I am glad to see you both alive."

Yomra chuckled. "You had so little trust in me? I am shocked."

"Benny, you shouldn't have come." Her mother shook her head.

"I had to, Mom. You two deserve to live your lives free and clear."

Her father was looking at her companions. "I see you have bound some men to your cause."

Tremble inclined his head. "We volunteered. She would not be safe alone."

Smith smiled. "We would not let her take the risk without us."

Argyle chuckled. "We went into it with open hearts and a single cause."

Yomra's voice was dry. "How sweet. Well, this is the closest thing to a family gathering I have ever had. What is the normal protocol?"

Harcourt Ganger raised his emerald-green head and glared at his great grandfather. "You thank us for coming and send us home."

Yomra laughed loud and long. "Oh, no. Now that I have you all here and see the obvious strength in your daughter, I believe keeping you here is the correct response."

The chairs snapped out cuffs and each and all of her great-great grandfather's guests were bound to their chairs by wrist and ankle.

The chairs elevated slightly, and Benny and her family were whisked away to a large room where there were no doors, no windows and no way out.

Benny's heart was pounding as the chair freed her. She ran to her parents and hugged them both. Her father squeezed her and then held her back with his hands on her shoulders. "A demon king, huh?"

She chuckled. "Did you expect anything else?"

Freddy barked, and Benny's mother picked her out of the bag, laughing as her face was licked frantically.

The tiny three-pound dog greeted both of the Gangers with enthusiasm.

Benny's father smiled slowly. "You brought Freddy here?"

Benny grinned back. "I brought Freddy here."

Freddy wiggled back to Benny, and Benny put her back in the purse. It was nice to have a friend who was portable now and then.

Harcourt looked at her entourage. "So, you have made it official."

Lenora laughed. "It is a binding spell. Well done, Benny."

"Thank you."

Her mother went from one man to another, hugging them in welcome. "Welcome to the family, boys."

Benny grinned when her father went over and shook the hands of her collection of demons.

Her mother whispered, "What is the plan, Benny?"

"Well, when you two were taken, I made a few calls and I chatted with Minny. She is going to start hauling us out of here in the next ten minutes."

Argyle scowled. "We have only been in the zone for three hours."

Lenora shook her head. "Time moves differently here. One hour is three in the normal world. You have been here for nine hours.”

“Right. We need blood from Yomra on the way out.” Benny rubbed her nose.

Lenora raised her brows in surprise. “Really?”

“Minny figured out a way to keep this from happening again. I think we should take advantage of all her hard work, don’t you?”

Harcourt chuckled. “If she worked something out, we would be foolish not to. Her pedigree is nearly as convoluted as yours, Benny.”

Benny grinned and turned to the agents. One by one, she kissed them and infused them with her strength. She had enough power with her to transport them all out of the demon zone, but she needed that blood to keep this from happening again.

Lenora held onto her husband and asked Benny, “What is the sign?”

"We are waiting for music and fire."

Her father gave her a serious look. "Do you have a plan for getting out of here?"

"Of course. You will know it when you see it."

Chapter Nine

It was easier to stand with Tremble holding her than by herself. His body heat sank into her, and his fey blood sparked the air with the scent of fresh leaves.

Benny stood with her eyes closed, waiting. The first note rang out, and she started to move.

"It's happening. We need to get ourselves to the street as quickly as we can."

She reached into the pocket of the bag and withdrew the scrap from the gown of the goddess of death. Benny stepped away from Argyle and wiped the wall in a wide arc. She tapped the fabric to the stone, and it shattered. She put the scrap back in her bag and lifted Freddy into her arms.

"Let's go. He will have felt that."

Their group surged out the door and headed for the dining hall. The path to the front door was clear, and the first words of Minerva's song were reaching them.

Yomra charged through the wall toward them, claws out. "You shall not leave."

Freddy growled, and Benny launched her through the air. Freddy went to full hellhound mode, three feet high and all teeth, wreathed with hellfire. She went for his leg and grabbed it, pulling him to the ground.

Argyle and Tremble held his arms down while Benny grabbed for the vial in her cleavage. Smith ushered her parents past them and toward the front doors.

It left her free to do what she needed

to do.

Yomra was fighting hard, so she grabbed the knife on her thigh and cut the blue skin at the elbow. His blood was sluggish, but she got a few drops into the vial before his skin closed. She sealed the vial and reached for another.

"Hold him." she stabbed into his side and collected more blood. "Damn, he heals fast."

Yomra was muttering at her in the demon language, and he hissed when she went in for a third strike. "This is going to have to be enough."

The third vial went into her clothing, and she looked her ancestor in the eyes. "Thank you for your help. I just need you to sleep now."

She held her hand over his nose and mouth, applying a sleep spell that should work on demons. It wouldn't hold him long, but it should give them the time they needed.

She kept her finger on his pulse, but it was his erection flagging that proved he was unconscious. She got to her feet and sheathed her knife. "Let's go."

Argyle smiled. "That was different."

Freddy resumed her more portable form, and Benny scooped her up. "Well done, Freddy."

Freddy yapped excitedly and wiggled in the bag.

Benny, Argyle and Tremble ran for the door. The other three were waiting at the door, and Minerva's song was getting stronger. A heavy rhythmic thudding was also getting closer. There were shouts of confusion and fear, which were not in keeping with the demon zone.

Harcourt opened the door, and he cracked one of the guards in the jaw while kicking the other. Benny had never seen her father in action, and she could see what Lenora saw in him.

The thundering grew louder, and

down the street, a wave of horses could be seen, flanked by fire.

Tremble gasped. "Where did those come from?"

Benny blinked. "They live at our place."

The first of the horses skidded to a halt in front of her. It nudged her in the chest, and she didn't waste time. She gripped the withers of its mane and pulled herself up and onto its back. Everyone else was doing the same, and when they were all mounted, the fire gathered them up and kept them from being pursued by demons.

They galloped through the main street, past the shocked demons occasionally visible through the flickering flames.

Yomra's blood was still scalding hot in the vials. Benny shifted, but she didn't move them. The last thing she wanted was to drop the blood that she had risked her life to get.

The pale horse under her had a familiar feel. She moved easily with it as it rounded corners and sped on the straightaways. The walk that had taken hours was accomplished in a matter of minutes with flames guarding their backs.

The gate loomed in front of them, and the horses poured on the speed. She could hear Yomra's howl behind them, and she held her breath as they passed through the gateway, with fire sealing it shut.

Minerva was sitting at a picnic table, sweating with a gargoyle next to her fanning her with his wings.

"Benny, did you get it?"

Benny dismounted and pulled the vial out of her bra. "I got three of them just in case."

"Excellent. Here is the salve." Minerva put it on the table and unlatched the top. She frowned and looked around. She pointed at a tree. "You, I need a stir stick."

A twig snapped off and came flying toward her. She caught it and set it aside. Minerva withdrew an empty vial, and she jerked her head at Benny. "Okay, spill."

Benny pulled the onyx and obsidian dagger, slicing her forearm. She filled the small vial and handed both it and Yomra's to Minerva.

Her friend stirred the two bloods into the salve, and then, she handed it to Benny. "Strip and put it everywhere."

Benny looked at the agents, and they grinned. With care, she set Freddy down on the ground and put the vials in the bag next to her. She used a spell to remove her clothing before smearing the goop all over her.

The tingle of being surrounded by magic was a little weird, but Benny kept going until she had covered everything, including the soles of her feet.

Minerva held her hands out. "From the beginning of this blood to the last vessel and all beyond her, this cuts the ties and leaves the power. None may call upon the binding of bloodline, forward or back."

Benny began to tingle, and she was lifted through the air. To her surprise, she could see the same happening to her father.

Fire burst into being around her, a hot violet that didn't touch her. She was slowly lowered to the ground as the fire flickered and burned out. Her father was sitting on the grass a few feet away.

He looked over at her. "I am free." He laughed and reached for her mom, pulling her down to the grass and covering her face with kisses. "I am finally free."

Benny leaned up on her elbows and giggled. Even naked and covered with salve, she felt good.

Minerva grinned. "You can get dressed now. The fire burned off the salve and your attachment to Yomra."

Argyle was holding his hand out to her, and she smiled when he removed his shirt, draping it around her and doing up the buttons. "I think you have engaged in enough magic for one night."

She smiled and leaned against him. "I would say it was enough for a lifetime, but that is exhaustion talking."

The pale horse shivered and stamped its feet.

Tremble cleared his throat. "The horses say they will take us home. I am guessing they mean the manor."

Benny nodded. "Home sounds really good right now."

She moved away from Argyle and walked to Minerva. She hugged her. "Thank you so much for today."

"That is what friends are for. You can

ask anytime. Well, any time after Wednesday. I still have that negotiation to take part in."

Benny squeezed her. "We need to go for coffee soon."

Minerva started to shiver, and soon, she was laughing. "Coffee would be great. I will call you after Wednesday."

"Please." Benny gave her a final squeeze before letting her go.

"Now, get going. You need to lock in that binding spell before dawn tomorrow."

"Or what?"

Minerva grinned. "Ask your mother."

Everyone was already mounted except for her. Freddy was sticking out of the pouch that Lenora was carrying. Benny hauled herself onto the back of the pale horse, and their herd wheeled and galloped out of the park.

Goblins were having cookouts all over the park, each fire a different colour.

Benny realised that Minerva had called in a distraction that kept their tinkering with the gate to the demon zone from alarming the locals. It was about the same time that she figured out where she knew her horse from.

She leaned over the pale neck and whispered, "You are looking wonderful, Pooky."

He snorted and poured on the speed.

When she looked back, Tremble's face was glowing with excitement. There was something about this predawn ride that was getting him all worked up.

Argyle kept looking east, and when they finally thundered to a stop in front of the manor, she dismounted to open the door for him as quickly as possible. Light was stroking the ground near the drive, and he made it inside before it struck with full force.

She didn't blame him. Being blinded by the sun wasn't any fun.

Benny stood in Argyle's shirt as the rest of her family made it into the house. The horses reared, plunged and headed for the open space behind the house.

Her parents held hands and headed upstairs for some privacy. Benny padded to the kitchen and made a pot of coffee.

Freddy hopped down the stairs with a wild look in her eyes. She transformed back to human in the doorway to the kitchen. "Dude, I just saw your parents naked...again."

Benny grinned and gestured for her to take a seat next to Smith and Tremble at the counter.

"Okay, who wants breakfast?"

Three hands were raised, and Benny sighed in relief. Things were finally getting back to normal. She scrubbed her hands and started making breakfast.

Freddy got up and grabbed dishes and cutlery. "Do you feel any different?"

"Lighter, if that makes sense, like I

just took off really tight underwear. I feel like I can breathe now."

She filled a sheet pan with bacon and slipped it into the oven. She crossed the room and pulled out a loaf of bread, popping four slices into the toaster before heading to the pan she was heating on the stove.

She took the orders for eggs and pulled the bacon out before buttering the toast and stacking it. Once the next batch of toast was in process, she cooked the eggs in rapid succession.

Breakfast was ready in ten minutes, and they were all sitting, sipping coffee and enjoying a well-earned silence.

There was enough bacon left for her parents when they came down, wearing robes and relaxed expressions.

Lenora came over and kissed Benny on the forehead. "How long will the binding last, Benny?"

Benny paused. "I think it is for life. I

would have to check the book."

Lenora paused. "The book?"

"Yeah, it has been a while since I had to do any potion making."

Her mother nodded but looked worried. "Which flask did you use?"

It seemed like an odd question. "The one with your initials on it."

Her mother grabbed her, hauled her out of the room and whispered frantically in her ear. When her mother had briefed her as to the ramifications of that particular flask, Benny's palms got sweaty.

There was no problem as long as she consummated the union within a week of drinking the potion. If she went beyond that, they would all experience agonizing pain and be completely useless until the joining was completed. It was better to lock in the union and take the pressure off.

She steeled herself and went to fulfill

a promise. "Smith, come with me."

He got to his feet with a curious expression.

She smiled. "I made you a promise."

He was at her side in an instant.

Chapter Ten

"What brought on this sudden decision?" Smith blinked as she unbuttoned his shirt. Her bedroom looked a little weird with a shifter in it but Benny was willing to get used to it.

Benny glanced up at him through her lashes. "First and foremost, I made you a promise in the demon zone. I hold to my word. Second, when you showed your demon, it was an incubus, so sex is high on your personal agenda. Third, my mother just informed me that the vessel I used for the spell was originally designed to enforce arranged marriages. It was the gag gift that they had gotten to make sure that she and my father left their studies long enough to consummate their union. If I don't have sex with all three of you in the next five days, we are all going to suffer."

She unbuckled his belt and stroked him through the fabric of his jeans.

He swallowed. "You seem to know what you are doing."

"My great grandmother is a succubus. I had a far more thorough introduction to sex talk than you could imagine." She stroked his chest and pulled his head down to her, kissing him and nipping lightly at his lips.

He growled, and she felt his hands on the shirt, peeling it away from her until his warm palms were stroking her skin.

She sighed and leaned into his hands as he familiarized himself with her skin. The shirt she wore soon hit the floor, and she was left in bare feet as he started to kiss the side of her neck.

Jessamine floated in, paused with her

eyes wide and floated back out again.

Smith lifted his head and made a face. "You still taste like whatever that was you were covered with. I think a shower is in order."

She smiled. "I do believe you need to be naked to properly shower."

He grinned. "I do believe you are correct."

She grabbed him by a belt loop and hauled him into her en-suite bathroom. The shower was large enough for four of them to stand in.

"All right, furball. Strip."

He chuckled and removed his shoes, socks, jeans and underwear. When all he was clothed in was glorious golden skin, she sighed happily.

She stepped into the shower and scrubbed her hair, her skin and, then, she asked the age-old question, "Will you wash my back?"

He was behind her with a shower puff

and a sincere desire to get every inch of her squeaky clean. When her back was clean, he turned her and went over her front with attention to all the details.

When he lifted her and pinned her against the shower wall with his body, she was more than ready for him to join her in the most basic of fashions.

He rocked into her over and over. She clawed at his shoulders when she came. Finally, he roared his own satisfaction a moment before he bit her to hold her still while his hips jerked. She hissed at the pain, but it was part of mating with a shifter.

A need for knowledge of his true name, his soul name, burned with the rest of her, inside and out. The spell caster within her needed the true name for protection and she wanted to protect him. She wanted to protect all of them.

When he let her go, she stroked the wet hair out of his eyes and smiled. "Can

I know your true name now?"

He blushed. "Andrew. William Eric Andrew Smith."

"Oh, those are good names for a mom to yell."

He laughed and eased her down the wall until she was on her feet. "They were indeed."

She stood, and she should have been woozy, but her bloodline was a little on the robust side. Kyria had once told her a tale of taking a regiment of warriors without once lying down, and while Benny wasn't proud of the comparison, she was ready for another lover.

She sighed and stroked his chest and neck, enjoying the feeling under her hands. "Okay, towels for everyone, and I will find a guestroom for you to crash in."

He sighed. "Will you join me?"

"Eventually. I want to join with Tremble before I get some rest though.

Will that bother you?"

"If you come in smelling of sex and my partner? Surprisingly no." He frowned as if the thought didn't disgust him. The confusion that crossed his face was adorable.

She laughed. "That is the binding spell. It makes you want to do what is best for everyone in the union. Even the other guys."

He wrapped her in a towel and draped another around his hips. He cuddled her against him as they walked back into her bedroom. He sat on the chest at the end of her bed and pulled her onto his lap, inhaling and exhaling against her neck. Being with her seemed to relieve tension in him, so she leaned against him and enjoyed the closeness with her mate.

William Eric Andrew Smith. She wondered what Tremble's name actually was.

An hour later, Andrew was tucked into a guest bedroom, and he was breathing evenly. Demon shifting was exhausting, and it had been his first time. He would sleep for hours.

Sighing softly, she closed the door and went down the hall, searching for Tremble. Her sundress swished around her calves with every move and it felt loud in the silence.

He wasn't upstairs, so she went downstairs and found him in the library talking softly with her father and looking at some of the demon texts.

Her father looked up and smiled. "Benny, you look rested."

She winked. "Close enough."

He walked away from the elf who was raptly poring over the text, and he came over to give her a hug. "Thanks for coming for us, Benny."

"You would have done it for me, Dad.

Have you talked to Grandpa yet?"

"I did. He mentioned that he felt something was different. Kyria has not been in touch with him yet, but he feels she will be if she can get out of the zone."

Benny blinked. "Oh, right. She used to leave, propelled by Yomra."

Harcourt shrugged. "She will find a way. She always does."

She leaned back in his arms. "Are you less green?"

He winked. "I am. I feel more like my old self. My father is experiencing the same thing."

Her grandfather had the curled horns of the demon scholar, the same as Tremble did when he was wearing his demon. Well, she supposed it was when he was wearing *her* demon, but it was his manifestation.

"I am glad. I hope that this doesn't screw me up with the XIA. They had just accepted that I was a demon blood with self-control. What are they going to think when I let them know that I have cut our family loose from the influence of the king of our bloodline?"

Tremble looked up from the book and stared at her with vivid dark rainbow eyes with slit pupils. "Don't tell them."

She left her dad and wandered over to him. "Why not?"

"They will re-evaluate you and demand the spell that was used to release you. I do not feel that the spell should fall into the hands of someone who has not been raised with the self-control that your family has embedded into you." He gave her a solemn look.

She blinked. "I get the feeling that you guys are going to be tested for demon influence a little more frequently."

He smiled slowly. "Unless they can prove exposure to a new demon, they have no grounds for testing us."

He closed his book and moved in on her.

Her father cleared his throat. "I will go and check on your mother and Freddy."

Benny was focused on the elf that was crowding her back to the study table. "Uh, Tremble..."

He nuzzled his cheek against hers, whispering, "Yes, Benny?"

"What is your true name?"

He moved his lips and exhaled his name against her mouth. "Gelendor. Gelendor Hurias Tremble. There are a few more names but those are the important ones."

She didn't have a chance to engage in witty banter. He kissed her and lifted her to the surface of the table. He pushed her dress up over her knees and stepped between them while he undid the buttons holding the front of the sundress closed.

When his hand slipped inside her dress and his long fingers closed over her breast, she arched into his palm. His other hand moved between her thighs, and she groaned when he slid two fingers into her, followed by a third a moment later. She was rapidly approaching orgasm when he pulled his fingers free and left her breast so that he could work at the closure of his jeans.

When his cock was free, he pressed her flat to the desk and nudged against her. He planted his hands on the table next to her and slowly thrust forward. When she slid back, he grinned and draped her calves over his forearms while he gripped her hips.

Benny gasped when he finally went as deep as he could, and she reached up to grip his arms as he started to move inside her.

His face was focused, but he was watching her. When she felt a curl of pleasure, he angled his hips and repeated the inner caress. Every time she gasped, he echoed the motion that had made her twitch. It was strange to be analyzed while having sex, but she was swept up toward release in a few sweaty minutes. She thought it would soon be over, but Gelendor kept her on the edge of release until she was thrashing on the table and hissing at him. She wanted to wrap her legs around him, but he was keeping her precisely where he wanted her.

Benny concentrated and clasped him with her inner muscles to trigger his own orgasm, but her elf simply paused before resuming the slow, even strokes that kept her on the edge.

When she heard herself begging, he bent forward and kissed her, pushing her legs back and grinding against her with slow circles of his hips that had her shrieking as the pulse of release took over.

The table trembled as he pounded into her rapidly until he held himself against her, jerking and shaking as he came.

He released her legs and lowered himself to her, giving her a sweet kiss.

Benny lifted her head and returned the gesture of affection.

He lifted his head and smiled. "I look forward to taking my time with you."

Benny stroked his pale hair away from his face and tucked it behind his pointed ear. "I look forward to that, too. Thank you for taking the hint."

"There is no reason for us to delay this. We agreed to join with you before we drank the potion, we agreed to work with you at the XIA and we testified that you had not used your demon nature to influence us. Agreeing to have sex with you was implied." He grinned.

She chuckled and ran her hands over

his shirt. "Next time, no clothing."

"Deal. And perhaps, I shouldn't have started this in front of your father."

She laughed. "I feel a certain amount of smug revenge. I have had to leave this very room many times for the same reason."

He brushed his lips against her cheek. "Your father has told me that they were hoping for this general outcome, though not specifically one that involved you risking your life."

She arched her hips against him, feeling the delightful presence still inside her. "They hoped for this?"

"For you linking with all three of us. Your pedigree has a number of species that find fidelity a bit awkward. Since we each represent a different branch of magic, it is sensible that you have multiple mates, and each of us has already received release from their own people in regards to social obligation. We were possibly the best choice of agents that you could have been with."

Benny chuckled and slid her fingers through his hair. "I think that is just my luck."

"Then, I am glad for your luck." He kissed her again and slowly rocked against her. It was a hypnotic feeling that she wanted to continue, so she wrapped her legs around him and let her senses take over.

She still had hours before Argyle would be awake enough to mate with, so why not spend some time bonding with another of her partners?

Chapter Eleven

After another meal with her family and Freddy had headed home, Benny crept into Argyle's room two hours before sunset.

She slipped out of her dress and crawled into bed with Argyle, nestling against his cool skin and idly playing with his crimson hair until she was relaxed enough to nap up against him.

Benny woke when cool lips moved over her neck, her shoulder and nipped at her breasts.

She grumbled and heard him laugh as he rolled her to her back and wove his fingers with hers as he continued to taste her. She whimpered when he neared her pussy and thanked foresight for taking a flame bath earlier. When his tongue stroked her, she gritted her teeth and whined.

She felt the cold press of his teeth against her while he lapped at her folds and delved inside. Her breath left her in rapid gasps as his temperature affected her in a way she hadn't anticipated. Most of her lovers to date had been warm blooded and hot when she got them naked. Argyle had the temperature of cool marble, and she wanted to feel him inside her.

His tongue was torture, his fingers slid along hers, caressing and binding at the same time. Her breathing increased in pitch, and she tensed against him, trying to push herself over the edge.

The cool slide of his tongue went on and on. He flicked at her clit and then burrowed himself inside her with gleeful enthusiasm.

When she was arched against him and her breath was caught in short pants, he moved his head and bit her inner thigh. The sharp prick of pain made her scream, but it also set her free. A rush of fire ran through her veins, and Argyle growled and released her limb before he slid over her and sank his cock in to the hilt.

She met him thrust for thrust. To her shock, she felt her teeth sharpening. His eyes glowed, and she leaned up to sink her teeth into his shoulder a moment before he did the same.

She felt a second wave of spasms beginning in her core, gripping him and causing her limbs to clench as she held on and tasted blood. He released her in what she could only imagine was surprise.

She snarled, released him and rolled him to his back with a burst of strength, riding him hard until he gripped her hips and held her to him while he quivered with tension.

His teeth were clenched, his neck distended, and he held her tight for close to a minute before he slowly relaxed.

She flexed her thighs and slid her hands up his chest until she was lying on him with her head on his shoulder. He wrapped his arms around her and stroked the sweaty curve of her back.

"I didn't get the chance, what is your true name?"

"Cairbre. My name is James Cairbre Argyle."

She blinked and leaned up on him. "Charioteer?"

He laughed. "Yes. How did you know?"

"I have a lot of old relatives who are still around today. I have had to take five ancient languages via tutors and have gotten three via spellcasting."

He smoothed his hand down her spine. "So, you are well educated."

"As long as you don't count an actual degree, yes. If you do, I graduated high school."

"Why didn't you complete college?"

She wrinkled her nose. "There was a demon-related incident and the XIA was cracking down on scanning for demons. I didn't have enough control at the time to hide that energy. It was stay home and study or get arrested and dumped into the zone."

"What did the assessors say about you when you finished your training?"

Benny smiled; he was the first one to really ask. "I was given a few bits of information. The first was that if I didn't display any demon characteristics, I would be able to act as the first trained mage on a team. The second was that because of my obviously slutty nature—being a demon and all—that I would be allowed to have intimate relations with my coworkers."

His hand paused. "You are joking."

"Nope. I am allowed to mess around with you and you with me. No one will bat an eye, and there will be no repercussions. We won't have to hide."

He wasn't breathing, but he chuckled. "That is a relief. Work will be work, but it is nice to know that I can grab you the moment the shift is over."

"Sure, as long as you are faster than Smith and Tremble." She chuckled. She stretched. "And with that, I need to go and get some rest."

"You can sleep here."

She shook her head. "No, you are getting up, and I need to be in my own bed."

He sighed. "True. Ah, well. Soon, we will be on the same schedule."

She nuzzled her cheek against him. "I look forward to it."

She gave herself a dozen more contented heartbeats before she levered herself up. "Okay. I have to drag myself to my room. You need to pry Tremble away from the texts. I had no idea he was such a fan of reading."

Argyle moved out from under her, and she tumbled across the bed. It was effective.

"You don't know any of us very well. That will change, but it will be a strange process. Just as I learned about your education restrictions today, we will continue to learn about each other as time marches on." Argyle got up and headed for the shower.

Benny ran the cleansing fire over her skin again, slipped on her dress and left Argyle's room to make her way down the hall.

Her own room looked horribly inviting, and when she entered it and a sleepy Smith rolled over, she closed the door, shucked off her sundress and crawled into bed with Smith curled around her. He tucked her against his body and breathed her in as she slowly relaxed in his arms.

Lions weren't supposed to purr, but a soothing rumble was coming from Smith. She was out in under two minutes.

Smith joined the others downstairs while Lenora Ganger made dinner with her husband's help.

Argyle looked at him. "She is asleep?"

He nodded. "She is. You two wore her out."

Argyle and Tremble shrugged.

Smith asked Lenora, "Did that satisfy the spell?"

She set a casserole of cheesy potatoes

on the table. "It should have. You won't know for sure until next Sunday. Damn. You guys don't have to work tomorrow, do you?"

Argyle shook his head. "We are waiting to be authorized to return to duty. It could be tomorrow, it could be in two weeks."

Tremble cocked his head. "I hope it is later. We need to find somewhere to live. She can't run from one of our homes to the next."

Harcourt cleared his throat. "Lenora and I have already done something about that. The dower house is being expanded and renovated for all four of you to live there. Well, five if you count Jessamine."

Smith blinked. "You are serious?"

The demon shrugged. "As serious as I can be. It should be done by the end of the week."

Smith sniffed. "You are losing your

demon scent. It is fading."

Lenora smiled. "It isn't fading; he is just gaining control again. He hasn't had that control since I..."

Harcourt lifted her hand to his lips. "It is a good thing, love. You are here, and I am more me than I have been since you were in hospital."

Smith could see the love between the two, and he admired the example that they had set for Benny. She had gotten used to the forms love could take and chosen to embrace the ones that were not parasitic but built up the partner. He did not doubt that she had seen far more than any child would want to, but she had come through it strong and loving with a great sense of humour.

Tremble asked, "How did she come by the name Beneficia?"

Argyle smiled, "In my community, it is the name of an assassin."

Lenora smiled slowly. "It is my mother's name, and she is still a vampire kill-er for hire."

If Argyle could have paled any more, he would have. "So, that is Benny's grandmother on your side?"

Lenora smiled. "She is. My grand-mother, Sabina, was near to term when she was crushed by a carriage, and she was offered a chance at life in the dark-ness. My grandfather made her take the offer; he could not bear to watch the life leave her."

Smith looked at her with wide eyes. "Her husband was a vampire?"

"No. Lord Hearther was the vampire that gave her life. She healed and went into labour. My grandfather was a mage who had many friends across many spe-cies. He called upon the vampire; my grandmother transformed and had my mother."

Argyle was shaking. "So, you mean to say that I have been bonded to the granddaughter of the Hunting Shadow?"

Lenora smiled. "Do they still call her that? I will have to let my father know. He thought it would blow over after a century or so."

Tremble smiled and tried to change the fixation of Benny's namesake. "So, who is Beneficia's husband?"

Harcourt chuckled. "Welgainer Mills, the forest lord."

Tremble put his head on the desk. "I should not have asked."

Smith chuckled. "Any shifters I should get nervous about?"

Harcourt shook his head. "My mother has passed. She was Lettice Norington Ganger."

Smith swallowed. "The Great Wolf. The one who created a lasting peace between all the clans, packs and prides on this half of the continent. We are so out-classed."

Harcourt shrugged. "You know that

Benny comes from exceptional bloodlines. You don't even want to know how extensive her medical education is."

From his head down on the table, Tremble mumbled. "I think I can guess."

Her parents stood proudly.

Smith could see the pride radiating from them. They were the product of a brilliant and terrible family, and they had created a brilliant and dangerous daughter. And he was one of three men who had basically married her. *Ah, hell.*

Benny woke up after two hours of sleep. Her body wanted to be up in the middle of the night, and she blamed Argyle.

She muttered to herself, brushed her hair and put on jeans and a t-shirt, running around barefoot was one of the bonuses to being home.

She brushed her teeth carefully. Blood in the gums was never pleasant to wake up to.

When she was clean and presentable, she headed downstairs. It smelled like meatloaf and cheesy potatoes.

Everyone was eating when she came in, and she quickly took a seat and started filling her plate.

Tremble smiled sheepishly. "Sorry for not waiting for you."

She scooped up some green beans and winked. "This isn't the first meal I have been late for, and it isn't the last. When you get into a spell, you can't stop just because dinner is ready. Well, you can, but it blows up in your face and one of your eyes glow." She chuckled.

Lenora laughed and rubbed Benny's shoulder. "It was terrible and funny at the same time. She nearly blew half her head off and her hair was standing straight up. It was a good thing that demons heal fast. In about an hour, she was fine except for the eye. She got control over it about a month later. It showed up on picture day."

Smith was amused. "How old were you?"

"Nine. I was trying to make a potion to make my spell book glow in the dark so I could work past my bedtime."

Tremble stared. "And you blew your head up?"

"I wanted to peek into the cauldron even though it said it needed to be covered for an hour. Apparently, the part that made it glow was also explosive." She shrugged and finished grabbing for food.

Benny ate with a ferocious appetite, and the guys looked at her uneasily. She chuckled and sipped at her water glass. "You have seen me eat tacos. How is this different?"

Argyle pointed out, "You bit down so

hard, you bent your cutlery."

She set down the fork, and she didn't see anything. With a blush, she grabbed the knife and straightened it. "Sorry. I really like meatloaf."

Lenora smiled. "I know, punkin."

Benny finished her food and sighed. She sipped at her water and looked at her mates. "What would you like to do this evening?"

Argyle looked at her with a smile. "I would like to see the portrait gallery. You apparently have some ancestors I have only heard of in myth and legend."

She looked at her mom. "Do you want help washing the dishes?"

Her dad winked. "I will help her."

There was going to be more than dishes worked on in the kitchen, so Benny bolted to her feet. "Portrait gallery. Right. Come with me, guys."

They were just about around the corner when her mother moaned.

Benny blushed and kept moving. "Damn. Not fast enough."

Chapter Twelve

The double doors pulled open easily, and she stepped forward, triggering the lights.

Argyle was standing next to her, and he stared at the endless line of portraits with wide eyes. "How long does this go back?"

"We start with the most recent and then head back at least five generations. There are more after that, but most of them have passed on."

Smith stared at her. "Most of them? There are some still alive?"

She nodded. "Oh, yeah. I have some going back far past the first wave."

The men looked at her, and she

sighed. "What?"

Smith cleared his throat. "We are just wondering what we add to the union. You have an extremely impressive bloodline."

Benny pinched the bridge of her nose. "I am not my parents, my grandparents or my great grandparents. Extrapolate that as far back as you like. I am me, and my instincts told me that you guys are the ones for me. I know the plural is a little off putting, but I know what I need, and I need you, all of you."

She was engulfed in a group hug, and instead of it being smothering, they surrounded her so that she was in the centre of the triangle.

It was the best place she could have thought to be, and she hadn't even known it existed seconds before.

When they let her out, she kissed each of them softly, and then, she inhaled. "Right. Well, you have met my parents. This is the after picture."

She pointed at the image of her father standing behind and holding her mother, all green with his head spikes. The precious nature of their connection was shown in her hands over his and the gentle manner in which he cradled her.

Benny sniffled. "This one always gets me. It is so sweet."

Argyle put his arm around her shoulders, and Smith's was around her waist. Tremble produced a handkerchief.

She blotted at her eyes and smiled. "Right. Sorry. The rest don't make me so weepy."

She stepped with her group to the next picture. "This is them before the change. Oh and that is me."

Smith whispered, "How old were you?"

"I was six when this was done. Mom and Dad had to hold me in that position, but you can tell I wanted to be somewhere else." She looked at little Benny and the hands on her shoulders. One elegant and feminine, one heavier with ink stains.

Tremble smiled. "You were adorable. I have a niece that glares at the camera like that."

Benny filed that away. "I hadn't thought to ask. What will your families think about this?"

Argyle shrugged. "My family is no longer speaking to me, though they do still exist. My clan will eagerly embrace a relationship with your family."

Smith nodded. "I feel certain that my pride will as well. I have three sisters, one of whom is married to the alpha."

Benny blinked. "Oh. Nieces or nephews?"

"Two of each." He grinned. "Hey, you are an aunty."

Benny swayed. She had never considered that she was gaining family aside from the guys.

She looked to Tremble. "You?"

"One sister, one brother. My sister has a daughter and that is the niece I was referring to."

She exhaled. "I am going to need birthdays and preferences for gifts."

They all grinned at her.

She asked, "What?"

Smith chuckled. "You treat family very seriously."

"Of course I do." She straightened her shoulders and turned to the next portrait.

"This is my grandfather Zephyr with his wife, Lettice. Zephyr was half demon, but he could flick back and forth fairly easily. And that is my wee little dad standing there with the serious face. Grandpa is a scholar demon, like you were, Tremble."

The men paused, and she kept going. "Lettice was born a wolf shifter, which was weird because neither of her parents were wolves, but we will get to them later."

Tremble asked, "Pardon me, but did you say I was a scholar demon?"

She stepped to the next portrait. "Yup. You were a scholar, Smith was an incubus and Argyle was a warrior. The horns I was wearing marked me as a high king if I went to the trouble of killing Yomra."

Tremble smiled. "You may have gotten those from Welgainer. I have heard he has an incredible rack of horns when he chooses to show them."

"Funny you should mention him." She pointed to the portrait. "Welgainer and his lovely wife, the dhampir, Beneficia."

Argyle went up to it and looked from Benny to the portrait and back again. "You have her eyes."

"So I have been told. The next portrait has my mom as a little girl."

The men were startled into laughing when they saw Lenora sitting in the antlers of her father's head looking every inch the forest god with a little girl perched on his head.

Beneficia was holding her husband's arm, and they were all laughing. Benny was a little sad that grandmother was wearing deadly weapons, even in the family moment. No wonder she was so stressed out.

"Did she always wear the silver blades?" Argyle asked with genuine curiosity.

"Yeah. She still does. She is not a lady you want to startle." Benny chuckled. "She still looks like that, by the way. She hasn't aged."

He blinked. "I look forward to meeting her one day."

"You will. We have regular family gatherings and even aim for a variety of holidays. Most of the parties are held here at the manor, but if there are too many attendees, we rent out *Ritual Space*."

Tremble asked, "Is that place still around?"

Benny nodded and moved down the gallery. "It is. Neadra Baxter is still the proprietor, and she gives our family preferential treatment. We put in way more magic than we take."

She paused in front of her father's grandparents. "This is Alberta and Andrew Norington. She had no powers, and he was a mage multi-shifter. She was my true one part human. Her and Haggard Mills." She wrinkled her nose. "He is down there a little further."

Tremble raised an eyebrow, "You only have the two humans?"

"Powerless ones, yes. The rest are all mages."

She smiled at her great grandparents.

"They were Lettice's parents. Both have passed on, without remaining behind. They left the world together."

The guys were silent as she walked to the next portrait. They looked at the image of Kyria and her mate with surprise.

Smith asked, "Why is she here?"

"She is my great grandparent and my dad's grandmother. Of course she is here."

"She tried to strip you of your soul," He was obviously struggling to understand it.

"But she was a good woman while I was growing up and that was what helped shape me into the very accepting soul that I am today. She taught me about what love could withstand and how there comes a time to surrender to fate." Benny smiled fondly at her mirror image.

She cleared her throat. "Kyria's mate, Milton Ganger, was a mage and alchemist. He lived to the old age of ninety-eight. She was forced to return to the demon zone when he died, but she kept in contact with her son and his son as much as she could. She couldn't stay in the human world if she wasn't bound to a mage."

She twisted her lips. "We don't have a portrait of her parents. I have no idea who produced her, aside from the obvious."

They continued through the portraits that included a pixie, a frost giant, Sabina the vampire with her husband the mage.

Tremble asked, "These go back centuries. How did you get them all?"

Benny smiled. "A spirit painter. This is my gallery. My parents each have their own. They thought it was important to know what I had come from and how blended my history was. There are books that are filled with stories that my parents had a soul copyist create. The history of everything in my veins is in this room."

Tremble cocked his head. "Where are the books?"

She laughed. "In the shadows near the door. They build up with my own activities, so you had better watch the dates on the books."

They finished with the portraits and entered the statue gallery.

Smith smiled at the woman sporting stripes in the arms of a man covered with designs etched into his skin.

"Why did they become statues?"

"They go back over a thousand years. Their names are etched in the base of the statuary. Their blood may be in my veins, but they don't come when we call. They still deserve to be acknowledged." She shrugged.

Argyle looked through the statues and came to a halt. "I know this woman."

Benny followed him through the statues and paused in front of the statue. "Ah, her. She is my godmother, Giltine. Lithuanian snake goddess of death, mistress of the poison of the dead."

Smith cocked his head. "Minerva gave you a scrap of Giltine's gown."

"She did. It opened the doors in the demon zone. Only something that was ancient power could work in the zone. Giltine has been generous with her assistance before. I can only imagine that Minerva got the scrap via polite and honourable means."

She bowed to the statue with her hand over her heart. "Her gift saved seven lives that will eventually come into her embrace."

The stone glowed softly in acknowledgement. Benny sighed in relief. She had called upon her godmother before on a day she didn't like to think about, but it was not something she would ever take for granted. Goddesses did not like to be taken for granted.

The men must have caught onto her mood, because they completed their examination of the statues and then requested that they return to the daylight.

Benny knew a good idea when she heard it, and they walked back past all the generations that led up to her existence and out the doors.

The moment they exited the gallery, her phone rang and she dug it out of her pocket.

Her aunt's number was displayed, and she blinked. "Excuse me while I take this call."

"Hello? Aunty? Just a moment."

Benny walked with her guys to the den and gestured for them to have a seat. She threw a silence spell around her and suddenly remembered why her aunt was calling. *Oh, hell.*

Chapter Thirteen

Benny had completely forgotten about the anniversary party until her aunt Sabina called her and warned her that arrangements were underway.

The ruby anniversary was a big one, and Benny couldn't believe that it had slipped her mind.

"Benny, the entire family knows that you have been busy. This is the beginning of your life and the celebration of theirs. We will handle everything, and you just have to show up with those three agents of yours."

Benny laughed. "Of course, Aunt Sabina. No sampling though. They are mine."

"Ever since Edgar died, I have kept my sampling to the necessary." Her aunt chuckled.

"Where are you now?"

"Over in Bright Larch, doing some clan business."

Benny was flailing around for a notepad with one hand while pinning the phone to her ear with the other. "What kind of clan business?"

"Oh, just touching base with the local king. Gaining permission to pass through his lands. I should be there in a few days. The caterer is booked, music, flowers, wine, beer and all the alternative refreshments are arranged. You just need to keep the secret and prepare to sing."

Benny blinked. "Sing?"

"We talked about this. You were going to sing a tribute to their relationship and their bond as a couple with you as part of their family."

"Right. Right. I wrote the poem, I just haven't set it to music yet. I have a few ideas and will get them hammered out by the party."

Her aunt laughed in low and throaty tones. "You will do fine, Benny. Beneficia has even arranged leave to come in for the party. It is looking like the majority of your living family will be there."

"Excellent. I look forward to seeing them all. Talking through the portraits just isn't satisfying. I need hugs." Benny grinned.

She had left a small detail out of her tour of the gallery. Talking to her ancestors who were willing to make the connection could most easily be accomplished via the portraits. A phone worked just as well for the living ones, but the dead ones were trickier.

She was delighted that Beneficia was coming to the party. Being the deadliest dhampir in existence, she required special writs to travel from one state to the next. An entire line of vampire kings had to sign off on her travel, and it took a bit of effort. That she was making the effort for her daughter was sweet. She was a loving mother, but she was also tremendously fun at parties.

"I will contact Neadra to confirm *Ritual Space* for the event." Benny crossed her fingers.

"Good. Confirm the address with me, and I will have all the arrangements set. We are running out of time, child. Call Neadra and call me back. The sooner it is arranged, the sooner we can relax."

"Yes, Aunty." Benny blushed.

"So, when will I meet these young men of yours?"

"At the party, but I should warn you that we have already been bound together. Even if you are not a fan of them, I am keeping them all."

Sabina paused. "I see. Well, when are

you going to hold your reception?"

"Um, we are going to have to finalize it with all of their clans, prides and folk."

"Fine, but the moment you have locked it all in, I want to hold a party for you. Set a date for the next full moon. Hang on."

Benny heard pages flipping. Her great grandmother still liked the feel of paper.

"Aha! You have eight weeks. The next blue moon. I think it will be appropriate, and it will give you plenty of time to get into your new job."

"How did you know about that?"

"I talked to your mother a few days ago." Sabina chuckled. "Okay, go make that call. I would do it, but Neadra doesn't like vampires."

"Right. I will call you soon, Aunty."

She disconnected the call and waved off the wall of silence.

"Gentlemen, I am about to have my ass handed to me by my aunty." She wrinkled her nose and headed over to the couch, settling between Smith and Tremble.

She scrolled through her contacts until she found the number she wanted. Wincing, she connected the call.

To her relief, the call was answered immediately. "Hello, Benny."

"Neadra, I have an emergency and I need to rent some space."

The low chuckle was extremely amused. "How much?"

"What do you have available for Saturday night?"

"Shockingly enough, it is wide open. You can have the whole place."

Benny blinked. "I will take it. Do you need a deposit or are you content to take my word."

"Do we need transport access available?"

"Please, beginning an hour before sundown until an hour after dawn. Caterers, tents and a sound license please."

"Done. Call me with the details in the morning. I was just on my way to bed."

"Thanks, Neadra, you are a life saver."

"Enjoy it. You lucked out. I just had a rash of cancellations with non-refundable deposits. With your booking, I am in a delightful mood."

Benny grinned. "Thanks again. I will get the details for the caterers and have it faxed to you in the morning."

"Anything for your parents, dear. I know what time of year it is. Good night, Benny."

The line went dead and Benny blinked at her phone for a moment before tucking it into her bra. "That turned out incredibly well."

"You are planning a party?" Argyle was warming his hands by the fire.

"We are. My parents have been together for nearly fifty years. We normally have a party here for their anniversary, but now, we are going to head out to *Ritual Space* and run around for a night. We will have the entire place to ourselves, so all family is invited no matter how freaky." She grinned.

"Are we invited as well?" Smith smiled a little shyly.

She leaned over and kissed him. "Of course. You are all expected to be there. I will send you the invitations sometime tomorrow...or later today. I am a little muddled right now."

Tremble chuckled. "Since Smith got a personal invitation, it is only fair that you will have to invite me and Argyle the same way."

She pressed her forehead to Smith's and rubbed back and forth for a moment before flipping back and landing in Tremble's lap. His kiss was rough, he held her hair and she responded for a moment before her reaction ceased his incursion.

Benny glared at him and licked her lips. "Will you attend my parents' anniversary surprise party?"

He inclined his head. "I will."

She sighed and boosted herself off his lap, sashaying over to Argyle. "Argyle?"

He grinned. "Yes?"

"Would you attend my parents' anniversary surprise party?"

She placed her hands on his chest and slid up the cool surface of his shirt, even with the fire, he was still cold.

She loved the combination of heat and cold as she went up on her toes and pulled his head down. His lips were soft marble, and she shivered against him. They kissed slowly and softly for several minutes before Smith growled low in his throat.

She leaned back and blinked as she waited.

"Of course I will join you. I will file a

request for the night off as soon as you let me go."

Smith and Tremble were already on their phones.

She sighed and let him go.

Benny fished her phone out of her bra, "Fine, you do that and I will call my Aunty Sabina."

Argyle stiffened. "I thought Sabina was your great grandmother."

"She is; she just prefers to be called Aunty, as does Beneficia." She hit her aunty's number and waited while it rang.

Sabina was a vampire; she would be awake.

"Hello?"

"Aunty Sabina, it's Benny. I have booked *Ritual Space* for Saturday night, and she is expecting a fax with the details. Transports will be allowed beginning one hour before sunset and continue to be accessible until one hour after dawn. She is getting the noise waiver, so we are good. We have the entire facility."

"How did you manage that with such short notice? I am not complaining, I am just amazed."

"It was pure luck." Something sparked in her mind about luck, and her eyes went wide.

"Right. Well, hooray for luck. Okay, I will fax her the information, and she can call me after sundown. I am emailing you a copy as well, so check it out and see if I missed anything. Just make sure to have the song ready."

"Yes, Aunty. All the invitations are out?"

"They are. You know the spell?"

Benny smiled. "I do. I will get to it as soon as I hang up."

"Thanks, pet. It was something I could never grasp after Beneficia arrived."

"No problem. Have a good night."

Sabina groaned. "Unlikely. I have to negotiate for possession of a few thralls. They went to a party and the king decided not to release them. My job is so glamorous."

"And you do it well. Good night, Aunty."

"Good night, Benny. See you in a few days."

Benny hung up and sighed.

Her guys beamed at her.

Smith chortled. "We all got the week and weekend off. I have no idea how we got so lucky."

Benny sighed. "I think we have Minerva to thank for that."

They looked at her in surprise.

"She gave us a thousand doses of luck in the binding spell. I think it has officially kicked in, though the first sign may have been the piece of Giltine's robe. The odds of her having that were astronomical."

Tremble put his phone away and walked up to her, wrapping her in his arms. "We are feeling exceptionally lucky, and this is enough proof that you are possessed of a powerful magic."

She sighed and rested her head on his chest. "And it is all human mage magic, so there will not be issues with you three being tainted by demon magic again."

Tremble chuckled. "They cannot test us for that for another year."

Instead of cuddling her, he spun her away from him and then back.

She went into the patterns of dance on instinct. "Why are we dancing?"

To her surprise, Smith took her hand and twirled her expertly. "If I am not mistaking your invitation, we are going to a party, and I don't think any of us will dance with anyone else."

She let Argyle take her for a spin after that, and then, she stepped back. "I have to write an invitation with addresses and details."

They sighed as one.

She went to the desk in the corner and opened a piece of parchment. The address was in her phone, and she prepared a quill, selected the proper ink and started to work the letters onto the parchment. She was careful with the dates and the spelling of the address. When she had it down and completed, she verified the spelling twice before chanting to wake the ink. When the ink lifted, she leaned in and blew softly on it. The words disappeared with her breath, and they were being printed on every invitation that was sent by Sabina.

When it was done, she capped the ink, put away the parchment and took the quill to the fire. When it flared blue, she relaxed.

Tremble was watching with fascination. "You use the magic so easily."

She shrugged. "I have learned it along

with learning to walk. It is my nature."

"I thought you would have more fey magic."

She smiled. "I have that too, but I don't use it in the house. I would blow the roof off by accident. My grandfather taught me, and he is a little heavy handed with the natural powers. I was not taught subtlety."

Smith looked a little unsure. "Is there a chance that I can go for a run?"

She blinked. "Damn. I am sorry. Of course. Come this way."

Benny led them out of the den and to the back of the house, past the kitchen and out to the grounds. The manicured lawns rolled, and Smith stripped rapidly, shifting into a stunningly proportioned lion that gambolled over the green before dashing to the left.

Benny turned to the other two. "Care to join me on the terrace? We can wait until he finishes chasing the horses."

Argyle grimaced. "Please pardon me, but I need to go and feed."

"Can you drink from me?"

His eyes glowed hotly. "I would love to, but I do not wish to weaken you."

"I am sure you will not take more than you need. You are a given vampire, you don't need much."

He nodded slowly as if afraid she would change her mind. He settled on a chair, and Tremble watched over them as she sat in the vampire's lap.

Argyle held her carefully, and he lifted her forearm to his lips. He licked the skin slowly, and she shivered. When he bit, she felt only a surge of heat and nothing more.

The heat began to build with every stroke of his tongue and each sucking swallow. She was shaking in his embrace, his hand behind her back supported her and the other kept her hand to his lips while he drank.

He drank for ten minutes or so, and then, he carefully licked her punctures closed. If Tremble hadn't been there, she would have stripped naked and jumped him after the first bite.

Her blood was singing, and she was lightheaded. When Argyle looked down at her, she grinned and kissed him, tasting her blood in his mouth.

She sighed when they parted. A moment later, she bolted to her feet at the sight of a lion being chased across the meadow by a herd of horses who looked distinctly unimpressed with the newcomer.

Tremble leaned against the railing. "You know what they are, don't you?"

"The horses and Pooky? Yeah. They are the wild hunt. Ancient steeds of the fey, and in alternate mythologies, they are the bearers of the dead." She grinned at his surprise.

"Tremble, my car can change into a

van and then into a horsy. I put that together already. Dang, I think I should head down there and calm things down."

With the pursuit heading back in the other direction, she stepped out into the path of the stampede.

Saving one's mate from a herd of horses because he tried to chase them didn't rank high on her dignity metre. The moment the lion passed her, she stepped out, and the herd split, thundering around her and Smith. She could feel his breath on her neck, and she glanced back at him. "You just had to try and grab them, didn't you?"

He rumbled and his tail lashed from side to side. To see a goofy and pleased expression on his features melted her heart. She stroked his nose and rubbed his forehead. "Having fun?"

He rumbled again and nuzzled her with his huge head. Argyle and Tremble came toward them, and she leaned against Smith's huge skull.

They stood around and scratched him behind his ears and under the thick waves of his mane for close to an hour. Smith was boneless with happiness when they finally decided to return to the house. Dawn was approaching and an uneventful sleep was definitely earned.

Chapter Fourteen

Benny woke up smooshed between Smith and Tremble. She didn't remember getting into bed with either of them, but here they were.

She levered herself up and out from between them. Tremble rolled to one side and clutched at his pillow while Smith frowned. With some contortions, she left the bed and headed to the bathroom to attend the call of nature and take a proper shower.

She was unsurprised to feel a pair of hands on her in the shower, but she was taken aback when she turned to see Argyle soaping her back. "Good afternoon."

He pressed a kiss to her shoulder. "Good morning. For some reason, I am wide awake this morning."

She whispered, "What time is it?"

"Eleven in the morning." He was running his hands over her and getting the soap into all the nooks and crannies that had seen so much action the day before.

"Ah. I thought it was closer to four."

He chuckled and ran his hands over all of her curves. "No. You must have some rejuvenating properties in your blood."

"I probably do. There are a lot of extremely long lifespans in my family."

He bent forward and pressed his lips to her neck. She arched back into the shower spray, and his cool mouth mixed with the hot water to make her shiver.

His hand worked between her thighs, and the hot spray, cold skin and precise touch of his hand had her gasping under the flow of the water until she bit her lip and clutched at him with her nails in his shoulders as she enjoyed her first climax of the day.

Dazed, she didn't move when he turned off the water and helped her out of the shower. She was still focused on her swimming senses. He tucked a towel around her, and she wrapped her hands behind his neck, pulling him in for a kiss and playing with his hair. "I do love your hair colour."

He chuckled. "I guessed as much. You play with it every time you are in touching distance, which is not as often as I would like, but that is something that will change as we settle down. I do love the way you taste."

She blinked. "Well, it is probably all the magic."

Argyle whispered in her ear, "That wasn't what I was referring to."

Heat seared her cheeks, and she cleared her throat. "How did you hear I was up, anyway?"

"Jessamine and I were working on the floor plan of the new house. She told me that you were up, and I can move quickly when I need to, though slow is my preferred pace." He winked.

Her blush didn't show any signs of slowing.

Smith and Tremble sat up when they came into the room.

Argyle sighed. "Well, I am going to have to leave you."

She blinked. "What?"

He laughed. "I need clothing, a toothbrush, my laptop. Jessamine said that the house is working on one large bedroom for all of us, but that won't provide me with what I need." He smirked. "Lenora did provide me with a set of sunglasses that will keep the light from blinding me, so I should be good to go."

Smith got up and pulled on his jeans. "Can you take me by my place?"

Tremble nodded. "Me as well. I would like to be back here for dinner."

Argyle nodded. "Come on. Get dressed. I will meet you downstairs."

Benny felt left out, but then, she had all of her stuff around her.

She wandered to her dresser and pulled out some clean underwear and a black t-shirt with a kitten with wings on it. She was going to drop the towel, but she noted the three interested faces.

"You can head downstairs. I will be down in a minute. We are going to have to work on finding a way to each get personal time, or we will drive each other nuts. Namely me." She wrinkled her nose.

Argyle smirked and headed for the door. "Oh, Benny, what is that tattoo on your right hipbone?"

She scowled and put her hand over her towel-clad hip. "A birth-control spell. Regular human drugs don't do much for me, so Minerva helped me design it."

Smith sighed in relief. "So, I don't have to make any awkward announcements to my pride when I introduce you?"

She shook her head. "No. I don't want to have to rush anything, and I will have quite the lifespan to deal with if I don't do anything stupid. I can spare a few years before kids are an issue."

Tremble smiled and came over to give her a kiss. "I would not mind a child."

She looked at him archly. "You would like to quit the XIA to look after the child full time? I have just gotten a job where I can be myself out in public. I am not going to put a cork in that until I have had some life experience that doesn't involve me hiding in the shadows."

He crossed his arms and gave her a bland look, all confidence and buff security. "I would certainly resign my position to take care of my child."

She blinked. "Well, that sucks the air out of my next statement, but good to know."

He gave her a quick kiss on the lips. "Think about it."

Smith pressed a kiss to her cheek a moment later. "I am content to wait a while."

She laughed and gave him a peck on the lips. "Me, too. Off you go."

Argyle didn't mention anything because he couldn't father a child. He merely winked and headed out of her bedroom and toward the stairs.

The other two bowed and left her alone. She sighed and pushed the door closed. With her mind whirling with the mental image of a small person in her arms with pointy ears and her hair, she got dressed and then pulled on a set of denim shorts. She put on her favourite kitten socks and pattered downstairs where her family was, once again, gathered in the kitchen.

She came to a halt when she saw her father. "Dad?"

He turned to her with open arms. "Come here, Benny." He hugged her.

She hadn't hugged her dad as a human for over sixteen years. The lack of scales was weird and his thudding heartbeat was in her ears.

"What happened?"

He grinned. "Now that Yomra has lost his influence, I was able to use a glamour again. It feels solid, but I am testing it out at home."

Her father's hair colour was a shade darker than her own, but his dark-hazel eyes were the same ones she saw in the mirror every morning. He was just as handsome and reassuring as he had been when she was small and he was lecturing at colleges and universities around the country.

"You look..."

He grinned. "I know, sweetie. It feels pretty good, too. My demon form is losing its ferocity, but this will be a better transition for going out in public."

She wiped tears off her cheeks. "It is just so nice to see *you* again."

Benny could see her mom, and Lenora smiled while she finished putting lunch on the table. It appeared that the change to the old was a favourite all the way around.

After lunch, the guys took off and went in search of a change of underwear. Benny was not complaining.

She saw her parents eyeing each other once they had finished the dishes, and Benny chuckled. "I am going to take a walk to the dower house. I will be back later."

Her parents didn't respond, so she

left out the back and started walking across the grounds.

Pooky galloped up to her and nudged her with his head. She grinned. "Fine. Let's go for a ride."

She hauled herself astride him, and he galloped off toward the dower house. Whatever was going on there, he was eager to have her see it.

They jumped the creek, crashed through the meadow and, finally, he jogged into what would be her back yard.

"Oh, wow."

The back deck that hadn't been there before had a huge hot tub large enough for all four of them to fit in easily. Benny walked into her home, and she noted that it was three times larger than it had been on the main floor. A gym had been added with heavy-duty machines, a larger kitchen and dining room took up the main floor, complete with a living space and a wide-screen television.

Benny snivelled as she walked up the stairs. Her parents and the house had gone above and beyond. She checked the guest bedroom, the upstairs bathroom and, then, she gingerly made her way into her own bedroom.

Her bedroom now took up two-thirds of the length of the house. Beds for the guys were arranged on one wall, but the focal point of the room was the bed that was wide enough for all of them. "Oh, geez. That is not happening."

The house around her sent a wave of amusement out.

The wardrobes were empty and ready. There were bookshelves waiting for books, footlockers and a pile of pillows on a thick carpet. The bathroom was built for four people to brush their teeth at the same time. It was a home built for her group, and Benny sighed. "Is there a study?"

Silent laughter ran through the walls around her. She headed down the stairs and followed the silent nudging to a flat and nearly invisible seam in the wall under the stairs. It opened at her touch, and a staircase spiralled down under the house.

She followed the spiral down into a space that made her cry like a toddler. In a wood-lined room that felt warm and snug. She had bookshelves, desks and her personal spell books in place. Across the room, a lab was fully set up behind a blast spell. It had the texture of water when she entered it but was bouncy as a marshmallow when she struck it.

There was a modest selection of ingredients and equipment, but it was more than enough for the standard alertness spells and healing potions that she made up for herself. Potions weren't really her thing, but it was nice to have the option to fiddle with it if she had the inclination.

She had her personal space. If she wanted to share it, she could, but if she wanted privacy, she had it.

"Thank you so much." She spoke to the house around her.

Her mom wasn't able to tell her when the family noticed that the homes were alive, but she suspected it had something to do with spellcasting. At home, Benny was fairly relaxed about using magic, as were her parents. That casual power must have seeped into the walls somewhere along the way. It was either that or the wood had been alive when the houses were built.

With one last, wistful look at the space around her, she climbed the stairs and let herself out the back door.

Pooky shook his head and turned, pawing at the ground. A huge stable was visible where an empty field had stood.

"Shall we take a look?"

She walked with Pooky at her side to the barn and looked around at the space for the entire herd as well as a curry-comb and brushes.

He nudged her to the care equipment.

"Can't I just run you through the car wash?"

He snorted, so she began the hypnotic process of brushing his hide while he stood with his eyes half closed. Dust and loose hairs flew for a few minutes, and then, it was all about taking care of the pukha who had come into the demon zone with his buddies to save her.

His mane was silky smooth and gleaming, as was his tail, by the time she finished.

She stopped and he stamped. "Dude, there is nothing left to do unless you want me to put braids in it."

Her arms were throbbing, and he looked at her with narrowed eyes for a moment before he nodded.

She put the gear away and asked him. "Take me back to the manor?"

He nodded, and she slipped onto his back; the door to the barn slid shut behind them. She held onto the well-groomed mane as he bolted with the speed of a thoroughbred across the meadow, over the creek and onto the manicured grounds of the manor.

She slipped off his back near the terrace. "Thanks for that." She patted his back.

He butted her chest with his head and then wheeled around to show his pretty hide to the others in the herd.

Benny shook her head and walked into the house, finding both her parents studying in the library. "Thank you, both. That had to have taken a lot of energy."

Her dad looked up. "We did it before the Yomra incident. If I had known what was coming, we still would have done it.”

Her mother smiled. “So, you like it?”

“Yes, but how did you know about...” She waved her hand vaguely to indicate the guys.

Lenora smiled. “Even your father could see the way they looked at you. Hell, even Kyria mentioned it to me.”

Benny sighed. “Well, I am exceedingly grateful. I wonder how she is doing.”

Lenora got up and came over to give her a hug. “We can wonder, and I think we might one day find out. If she got free of Yomra, she might be with her mage and trying to have that family she has always wanted but been denied.”

Benny’s dad got up and joined the family hug. For that one moment, they were together with fond memories of the succubus that had gotten them to this moment.

Chapter Fifteen

oving into the house was going to have to wait until after the party. Benny got dressed and finished fussing with the bow on the gift.

What could a girl get parents that had been together for five decades? The box contained charms that she had put together with Tremble's help. The vines that surrounded the wedding-day images were made of minerals, wood, gems and iron. They were the most powerful protection spells she could manage, and friends and family had donated the materials. The photo of their first kiss as man and wife was in a spiral of magic and love.

Benny slipped the present onto her pocket and prepared to take her parents out for *dinner*.

She came downstairs and smiled at Harcourt and Lenora Ganger. "Are you two ready?"

Her mother was wearing an elegant midnight velvet gown, and her father was wearing a tuxedo that suited him admirably.

"You both look amazing." She brushed at her tears when her mother took her father's arm.

"Thank you. Now, where are the boys?" Lenora insisted on calling them that, even though Argyle and Tremble were older than Lenora was.

"They are finishing moving into the house. They are going to meet us at the restaurant." Benny smiled brightly. "Come along. Pooky has something special for tonight."

They left the manor together, and the

stretch SUV in the drive revved the engine.

The door opened, and her father helped her inside where she started the illusion spell.

Her mother smiled brightly, and her father settled next to her in the large space in the back of the vehicle.

"Anytime you are ready, Pooky."

The door closed and the vehicle rolled forward, down the drive and toward the highway.

When they pulled even with the house, there was a flash of magic and Benny asked, "Pooky, can you stop for a minute? I need to get my wrap from the house."

The SUV rolled to a halt, and Benny got out of the car, winking at the gathering of folk who were waiting to surprise her parents.

"Dad, can you come out here?"

He appeared a moment later, and his

face was shocked and, then, he grinned. "Lenora, Benny can't remember which shawl matches her dress."

Her mother left the SUV and the gathering shouted, "Surprise!"

Over two hundred people had gathered, and Benny was delighted that she had managed not to blow it.

Lenora was crying and holding onto Harcourt. Benny went up to them and smiled. "Happy anniversary."

Her mother grabbed her in a tight hug and squeezed. "Well done, Benny. I didn't suspect anything until that last flicker."

Benny chuckled. "Come on and meet your friends and family. Fifty years ago today, you two agreed to spend the rest of your lives together. Most of these folks were there."

Her parents grinned and wandered into the crowd, accepting hugs of congratulation and many comments on

Harcourt's changed appearance.

Benny sighed and headed toward Argyle. He was looking devastating in a tuxedo, as was Smith. Tremble was rocking a fey formal costume. He was covered in a black tunic, tight black trousers and about three pounds of silver embroidered thread. He looked delightfully sexy.

Benny kissed each of them lightly and smiled. "Have you been having fun?"

Smith grinned. "There are leaders here from nearly every high family on the continent."

Benny shrugged. "My family gets around."

From behind her, she heard, "Benny!"

Benny turned, and a blond with her hair in an elegant twist that belied her appearance of youth immediately hugged her.

"Soph! You look...fourteen."

Soph smiled at her. "Part of the curse.

You look great. Are these yours?"

Benny stifled a snort as Soph waved at the guys.

Benny made the introductions. "These are my mates. This is Argyle, Smith and Tremble."

Soph bobbed a curtsey.

"Gentlemen, this is Sophia DeMonstre, the Cursed One." Benny inclined her head.

Soph exhaled. "That is my least favourite part of the curse."

Smith raised his brows. "Curse?"

Benny explained with a grin. "Soph is part of a family that was cursed by a dying monster. She has to hunt and unravel curses that pop up randomly or are cast into objects. Her skill is to see the solution; her curse is to have to deliver it. Slow aging is part of the curse; she is older than I am."

Soph made a face. "Funny. Well, I am here with my parents, and they would love it if you said hi. And I am only older by a month."

Benny hugged her again. "I will be only too happy to say hello when I spot them."

Soph leaned in. "Are you singing?"

"With this crowd? Of course."

Soph bobbed another curtsey to the guys, and she took off, with the bounce in her step that was uniquely her.

Argyle blinked. "There was something very odd about her."

Benny grinned. "With a look from those green eyes, she pulled apart the magic that animates you. She analyzed Smith's shifting and took in Tremble's grasp of natural energies. She analyzed me once, and then, she got a headache. Minerva made her so dizzy, she vomited."

Tremble smiled, "I thought you had a more diverse bloodline than Minerva does."

"I do, but hers was far more powerful when it intersected with humanity. I am like looking at a starry sky. Minerva is like staring into the sun."

She looked around and linked arms with Tremble and Smith. "Come on, let's mingle."

They met with dragons, gargoyles, vampire kings, her namesake, the forest lord and Sabina. When Benny was ready to introduce them to her grandfather on her father's side, Sabina whispered, "You need to start this now."

Benny blinked. "I am the MC?"

Sabina took her by her shoulders and pushed her toward the stage. "Can you think of anyone better?"

Benny made a face and got up in front of the microphone. Her parents were ushered to a table on an elevated dais so that they could see the festivities.

The band concluded their soft song, and she nodded to them in thanks. She leaned over to the guitarist. "Do you have the song?"

"When you introduce it, we will play it."

She gave him a thumbs-up, and he responded with all four of his. She licked her lips and turned to the microphone.

"Thanks one and all for being here tonight for the fiftieth anniversary of Agatha Lenora Mills Ganger and Harcourt Emile Ganger. Fifty years ago tonight, they pried themselves away from their books and stood up in front of family and friends with a judge officiating, and they swore to be together until death did they part, for better or for worse, in sickness and in health. The richer or poorer thing wasn't an issue."

The crowd laughed. The Ganger family was ruthless when it came to investing, and they had enough money for ten more generations.

"They skipped along together for a

few decades before they realised that all of their friends' kids were in college and they hadn't bothered to start a family. I came along as scheduled."

More laughter rippled through the group. Benny watched her parents holding hands and smiling at her.

"There was another decade of lectures, tours, students and a child at home setting fire to dandelions in the yard. That is when the *in sickness and in health* came in. My mother got sick, really sick. Cancer is a bitch, but with all the magic in the world, we couldn't stop it. Harcourt really, really tried."

The crowd was quiet. Most knew what had happened next.

"Mom got sick, and Dad stayed at her side. Even at ten, I knew that death was about to part them. To my surprise, my mom lived and Dad turned into the emerald-green goof most of you are familiar with. They shared a soul, but as any of you realise, who truly know them...they always did. Here is to fifty more years of light, laughter and mayhem that always sees you side by side."

A server brought her a glass of white wine. "To Lenora and Harcourt! Fifty years and counting!"

The toast was carried through the gathering, and everyone raised their glasses to the happy couple. Benny drank, and everyone followed suit.

The conversation rose to a murmur, and Benny got a glass of water. She slugged down the water and faced the mic again. She nodded to the bandleader, and they prepared to get going.

"Mom, Dad, I wrote you a song about your life and the love that you showed me was possible."

She nodded to the band again, and then, she began to sing.

Benny felt the jerk as something

pulled her out of her body. Everyone seemed frozen in time, but she could hear her voice singing the song of love and loss and love again.

A figure in white at the edge of the crowd beckoned her over.

Benny felt her astral stomach flip. When she was standing in front of the woman, she curtsied deeply. "Lady Giltine. You honour our gathering."

A touch on her shoulder brought her upright again. "Little Beneficia. I see you didn't tell any of your part in your mother's recovery."

Benny blinked. "I didn't do anything. My father shared his soul."

"Your father shared his soul with your mother the day that he married her. Did you never wonder why I was chosen as your godmother? A goddess of death is not a normal choice."

Benny glanced at the woman in white with the pale-blue eyes that had seen so much. She was the death licker. Master of poisons.

"I did not think about it. I was not consulted at the time."

The woman smiled slightly. It was tiny, but it was there. "True. Your mother had been dying for two years when you were born. They bound you to me in the hope that you would do what you did. You stopped me in the hallway and kept me there until your mother had been revived as a demon thrall with half a soul. Because of our connection, it had to be me to collect Lenora, and with my goddaughter standing in my way, I could not progress without destroying what I had sworn to protect."

The day came to her. Her father and mother had told her to leave the room and keep everyone out. Benny had agreed and faced down the lady of death who tried to pass. She kept her *there until her father had opened the door with her mother, pale but breathing in his arms.*

"The demon venom killed the cancer and it killed her, but without a true death, she was able to be revived with magic in a way that should not have been possible."

Benny blinked and looked at the glowing faces of her parents listening to her sing. They both had tears in their eyes, but they were smiling.

Benny steeled her spine. "We are honoured you have come to our party."

"I was invited, but I wished to speak with you. Your men, do you wish to keep them all?"

Benny blinked. "Of course."

"Mark them as yours. Get your friend Minerva to help. She has creation in her blood. Mark them soon. Not all deaths are as easy as mine." She changed the direction of her conversa-

tion. "It is a lovely party. Thank Sabina for the invitation." Giltine faded away.

Benny finished the last line of her song, and it hung in the air.

Her parents began clapping frantically, and the crowd followed. She bowed her head for a moment while the noise roared, and when it ebbed, she leaned forward. "I would also like to thank Neadra for hosting this event here in *Ritual Space.* It was pure luck that I managed to get this place to ourselves, so feel free to zap, shift and do what you like as long as you respect the guardian of the property. Now, dance!"

Music kicked into life, and Benny headed down the stairs, across the open space and up to her parents. She handed them the box and smiled. "Here you go."

Her dad opened the box, and he stared in amazement at the charm. "Benny, this is wonderful."

Lenora picked hers up, and she teared up. "Oh, Benny, this is amazing. So much power."

"It is a specific protection charm. It can't be stolen."

Her father helped her mother put her charm on, and then, he put his on.

"Happy anniversary, you two. I love you both."

Her parents rose and came around the table to hug her. Her father whispered, "Thank you, Benny."

Benny looked over the dance floor and found Minerva, fidgeting near the edge. Benny smiled and worked her way through the crowd. "Minerva. I am so glad you could make it. I need to commission you for something."

Minerva looked exhausted.

Benny paused. "Geez, Minerva. Come with me."

Her friend was so tired that she followed.

The buffet was set up, but few folks were indulging. When they were away from the crowd, Benny sat her down on a stone and asked, "What is wrong?"

Minerva rubbed her forehead. "I think I taunted the wrong guy."

"Tell me about it."

"I don't want to, not today." Minerva straightened her shoulders and looked attentive. "What do you need?"

Benny waved it away. "I need a way to mark all of us; I mean me and the guys. Wedding rings won't really cover it. I need a tattoo or something, something that will work on all of us."

Minerva smiled. "I have something in mind, but it might be painful. Small but painful."

"Pain doesn't matter. Pain is fleeting. If it protects them from whatever is coming, I say that I can convince them."

Minerva grinned. "I bet you can. I will bring you the designs in three days. It will take that long to work up the ink, though I have the pattern in my head."

"Tell me what you want in return."

Minerva smiled. "One favour to be granted at a later time that will not cost you life, limb or the affections of your mates."

Benny smiled. "Deal."

They chatted about the guests at the party until the guys came to grab Benny for dancing. The logistics of dancing with all three were difficult, but not impossible. She spun and whirled until she was dizzy, secure in the knowledge that she was safe, her parents were safe and she was loved.

It wasn't a bad haul for a week of vacation. She wondered what the next week of actual work would bring.

Revisiting Benny has been such fun. In the next book, *Three Parts Fey*, Benny has to work through all the formalities of mating with three different social groups.

The vampires are going to be the easiest group to get a blessing from and that is all I am saying for now. ;)

Look for *Three Parts Fey* Sept. 1, 2015, and in 2016, the *An Obscure Magic* series will return with *Ritual Space*.

Thanks for reading,

Viola Grace
viola@violagrace.com
http://www.violagrace.com

About the Author

Viola Grace (aka Zenina Masters) is a Canadian sci-fi/paranormal romance writer with ambitions to keep writing for the rest of her life. She specializes in short stories because the thrill of discovery, of all those firsts, is what keeps her writing.

An artist who enjoys a story that catches you up, whirls you around and sets you down with a smile on your face is all she endeavours to be. She prefers to leave the drama to those who are better suited to it, she always goes for the cheap laugh.